THE LEGEND OF
SKELETON MAN

Also by Joseph Bruchac

Bearwalker
The Dark Pond
Night Wings
Whisper in the Dark

THE LEGEND OF

SKELETON MAN

A TWO-BOOK COLLECTION

JOSEPH BRUCHAC

HARPER

An Imprint of HarperCollinsPublishers

The Legend of Skeleton Man

Skeleton Man
Copyright © 2001 by Joseph Bruchac

The Return of Skeleton Man
Copyright © 2006 by Joseph Bruchac

ISBN 978-0-06-274768-6

Typography by Michelle Taormina
18 19 20 21 22 BRR 10 9 8 7 6 5 4 3 2 1
❖
First Edition

To my grandkids—Carolyn, Jacob, and Ava—who are none the worse for having stories such as these to grow up with.

CONTENTS

THE RETURN OF SKELETON MAN

THE BARE BONES OF SKELETON MAN

I'm sure you've heard the expression about a story "writing itself." In the case of *Skeleton Man* and *The Return of Skeleton Man*, it was not a cliché but my actual experience. I woke up one morning at 6 A.M. with the voice of Molly, my main character, in my head.

"I'm not sure how to begin this story. For one thing, it's still going on."

I went into my study, turned on my computer, and started to write as she told me how her parents had disappeared, and how a frightening stranger claiming to be a relative had become her guardian. It felt as if I was taking dictation.

After I'd been working for what seemed like a few hours, my wife, Carol, leaned her head in.

"Are you going to eat?" she asked.

"No," I said, still typing. "Thanks. But I'm okay skipping breakfast."

"Joe," she said, "I'm talking about dinner. It's now 7 P.M."

I wrote over sixty pages that day and finished my first draft in a week. And while it would go through numerous revisions, the basic terrifying story that Molly told me remained the same.

But why would I want to tell scary stories about monsters? Just to frighten those who heard or read them? No, there's much more to it than that. In all of our Native American cultures throughout the continent, such tales have always served more than one purpose. Rather than just being terrifying—and many of them truly are that, featuring cannibal skeletons, giant bloodthirsty beasts, and all sorts of malevolent beings—they also are meant to be instructive and even empowering. In my stories that draw on that tradition, I try to do the same thing.

I grew up fascinated by these tales and have continued to hear monster stories over the years. I shared them with my sons who then became storytellers themselves. I cannot think of a time when such stories have not been a part of my family's life.

One thing that all those tales had in common was that they were lesson stories. They weren't scary for scary's sake. The fact that they were frightening made them all the better for teaching. So what lessons could be drawn from them?

First, the simple truth that children (and adults) need to be aware of danger. Danger is all around us. It could be in the form of a natural disaster, a person meaning to do you harm, or even as a result of your doing something as foolish as crossing a road without looking both ways. If you are aware of all these dangers, you may be better able to avoid them or at least know what to do when confronted by a threatening situation.

Second, in many of our stories—such as the Haudenosaunee (Iroquois) tales of the Stone Giant—the threatening being is huge, powerful . . . and really stupid. That monster is inevitably defeated by a child, the Seneca character Skunny-Wundy—who uses his wits. By staying calm and using good sense, a child might be able overcome even the scariest of monsters. (Although, on the other hand, if you panic or do something unwise, the monster might eat you.)

Third, some of our worst monsters—such as the Algonkian cannibal known as the Chenoo or Kiwakw—were once people who were turned into monsters because they were consumed by their own greed and selfishness. The wind of winter then blew through them and turned their hearts into ice, filling them with a terrible hunger that could never be sated. That monster is meant to show how *not* to behave. In one variation of these types of stories, a Chenoo is transformed back into a human by a young woman who does not try to run away but greets the monster as a grandfather and melts its icy heart by feeding it hot soup.

Fourth, if you want to teach a lesson, you need to make it interesting. A story about learning to respect your elders might be boring, but a story about your elders turning into monsters and eating you if you don't respect them really drives the point home. Monsters kind of make everything more interesting. Our traditional storytellers understood and still understand that. If you want to get a child's (or an adult's) attention, start talking about monsters.

That's the cultural background in which my two novels exist. They're meant, like those traditional stories of my childhood, to be both interesting and instructive with the teaching aspect seeming so secondary a listener or a reader may hardly notice that she or he is being taught something.

Looking back on the experience of writing these two books, I can understand why these books shaped themselves as they did. Their overall arc is that of a traditional northeastern Native American story and both of my novels include traditional monster stories within them that influence the narrative and also act as a guide for my protagonist.

That Molly would be a strong female character is also no surprise considering several facts. In our northeastern Native cultures, we view women—and girls—as being just as strong as (if not stronger than) any male. Further, among the Haudenosaunee, it is the women who traditionally own the households, head the families, and choose the chiefs. A man who does not listen to the women of his family, I've been told by many contemporary Native men, is a fool. Also, there is a consistent theme in traditional Native American stories of women being brave protagonists. They save themselves from danger—quite the opposite of European tales of damsels in distress.

Having said all of this, it still comes back to how these books began. Not with an outline or an idea, but with a voice, the strong, resourceful, aware voice of a young modern Mohawk woman wanting me to tell her tale. I'll always be glad that she chose me to do it. Nyaweh, Molly. Thank you.

—Joseph Bruchac

SKELETON MAN

FOOTSTEPS ON THE STAIR

I'M NOT SURE HOW to begin this story. For one thing, it's still going on. For another, you should never tell a story unless you're sure how it's going to end. At least that's what my sixth-grade teacher, Ms. Shabbas, says. And I'm not sure at all. I'm not sure that I even know the beginning. I'm not sure if I'm a minor character or the heroine. Heck, I'm not even sure I'll be around to tell the end of it. But I don't think anyone else is going to tell this story.

Wait! What was that noise?

I listen for the footsteps on the stairs, footsteps much heavier than those an elderly man should make. But it's quiet, just the usual spooky nighttime creaking of this old house. I don't hear anyone coming now. If I don't survive, maybe they'll all realize I should have been taken seriously and then warn the world!

Warn the world. That's pretty melodramatic, isn't it? But that is one of the things I do well, melodrama. At least that is what Ms. Shabbas says. Her name is Maureen Shabbas. But Ms. Showbiz is what we all call her, because her main motive for living seems to be torturing our class with old Broadway show tunes. She starts every day by singing a few bars of one and then making it the theme for the day. It is so disgustingly awful that we all sort of like it. Imagine someone who loves to imitate Yul Brynner in *The King and I*, a woman with an Afro, no less, getting up and singing "Shall We Dance?" in front of a classroom of appalled adolescents. Ms. Showbiz. And she has the nerve to call *me* melodramatic!

But I guess I am. Maybe this whole thing is a product of my overactive imagination. If that turns out to be so, all I can say is who wouldn't have an overactive imagination if they'd heard the kind of stories I used to hear from Mom and Dad?

Dad had the best stories. They were ones his aunties told him when he was growing up on the Mohawk Reserve of Akwesasne on the Canadian side. One of my favorites was the one about the skeleton monster. He was just a human being at first, a lazy, greedy uncle who hung around the longhouse and let everyone else hunt for him. One day, alone in the lodge, waiting for the others to come home with food, Lazy Uncle burned his finger really badly in the fire and stuck it into his mouth to cool it. "Oooh," he said as he sucked the cooked flesh, "this tastes good!" (Isn't that gross? I love it. At least, I used to love it.)

It tasted so good, in fact, that he ate all the flesh off his finger. "Ah," he said, "this is an easy way to get food, but I am still hungry."

So he cooked another finger, and another, until he had eaten all his fingers. "Oooh," he said, "that was good, but I am still hungry." So he cooked his toes and ate them. He cooked his feet and ate them. He cooked his legs and ate them. He cooked his right arm and then his left. He kept on until he had cooked his whole body and eaten it, and all that was left was a skeleton. When he moved, his bones rubbed together: *tschick-a-tschick-tschick-a-tschick*.

"Ah," he said in a voice that was now just a dry whisper. "That was good, but I am still hungry. I hope that my relatives come home soon."

And when his relatives came home, one by one, they found that the lodge was dark except for the glow of the cooking fire. They could see a shadowy shape beckoning to them from the other side of the fire. They could hear a sound like this: *tschick-a-tschick-tschick-a-tschick*.

"Come in, my relatives," Skeleton Man whispered. "I have been waiting for you."

One by one all of his relatives came into the lodge. Skeleton Man caught them and ate them, all but one. She was his niece, and she had been playing in her favorite spot down by the river that flowed through the gorge. She was late coming home because she had seen a rabbit that had fallen into the river. She had rescued it from drowning and warmed it in her arms until it was able to run away.

When the little girl came to the lodge, she was surprised at how quiet it was. She should have heard people talking and laughing, but she didn't hear anything. Something was wrong. Slowly, carefully, she approached the door of the lodge. A strange sound came from the shadows within: *tschick-a-tschick-tschick-a-tschick*. Then a dry voice called out to her.

"My niece," Skeleton Man whispered. "Come into the lodge. I have been waiting for you."

That voice made her skin crawl. "Where are my parents?" she asked.

"They are here. They are here inside," Skeleton Man whispered. "Come in and be with them."

"No," the girl said, "I will not come inside."

"Ah," Skeleton Man replied in his dry, thin voice, "that is all right. I will come out for you."

Then Lazy Uncle, the Skeleton Man, walked out of the lodge. His dry bones rubbed together as he walked toward the little girl: *tschick-a-tschick-tschick-a-tschick*.

The girl began to run, not sure where to go. Skeleton Man would have caught her and eaten her if it hadn't been for that rabbit she'd rescued from the river. It appeared on the path before her.

"I will help you because you saved me," said the rabbit. "Follow me."

Then the rabbit helped the little girl outwit Skeleton Man. It even showed her how to bring everyone Skeleton Man had eaten back to life.

My mom and dad told me stories like that all the time. Before they vanished. Disappeared. Gone, just like that.

I was on TV when they disappeared. You probably saw me on *Unsolved Mysteries*. The news reporter said into her microphone, "Child left alone in house for over three days, terrified, existing on cornflakes and canned food." Actually I went to school on Tuesday and called out for pizza once. Mom had left money on her dresser when they went out that Saturday evening and never returned.

I didn't know they hadn't come back until Sunday. I had gone to bed Saturday evening, expecting them to wake me up when they came home, like they always did. But not this time. When I woke up that Sunday morning, I knew something was totally wrong. The house was quiet. Usually my parents were both up way before me. I should have heard Dad in the kitchen, banging the pans around. Sunday was always his day for making breakfast and he made a big thing about it. He'd thaw out a whole quart of blueberries from the freezer and warm up some real maple syrup. But no noise came from the kitchen, no pans rattling, no seventies music playing on the kitchen CD player—my dad is a freak for the Eagles and says it is impossible for him to cook without them.

I sat up in bed and held my breath. No rhythmic pounding of my mother running in place in their bedroom down the hall. I looked at the clock—eight thirty. By now Mom should have been halfway through her first set of aerobics, but there were no sounds of thudding sneakers. The only thumping I could hear was my own heart.

Maybe they'd been out so late that they were still sleeping. It had to have been late when they came back because I'd finally drifted off to sleep after midnight, waiting for them.

I stood up and went out into the hall. "Mom? Dad?" No answer.

It seemed to take me forever to reach the door to their room. It was like I was walking underwater. The door was only half shut. I pushed it open, not sure what I'd see. Maybe they'd jump out at me and tickle me and laugh at their joke.

But no one was there. Their bed hadn't been slept in. No one was behind the door or in the closet or anywhere. Not there in the bedroom, not anywhere in the house. And the car was gone from the garage. There was no sign of anyone. It was a cold gray day, as gray as the long driveway leading down to the road. I didn't go outside to look around. I could tell it was going to rain soon. I didn't go to a neighbor's house because I couldn't. We live out in the country without any neighbors anywhere near us.

It was freaky, that's for sure, but I wasn't scared. Not yet. I just felt it in my bones that they'd be back. I went into the living room and turned on the TV, waiting. I have no idea what I watched, even though I sat there for hours. I don't know if it was sports or cartoons or the home-shopping network. For some reason I never turned on the news, even though it might have had something on if they'd been in an accident. But that couldn't be it. Someone would have come to the house to tell me, or there would have been a phone call. I looked at the phone, hoping it would ring and praying it wouldn't.

Rain began to hammer at the windows at about noon, and I went around the house making sure they were all shut. I looked out my bedroom window at Dad's toolshed. Its one window was shut, and I was glad about that. I didn't want to go outside in that cold rain.

Finally, at about two in the afternoon, I decided I'd make breakfast. I set the table for the three of us, got out the juice and syrup and blueberries and milk and everything, even napkins that I folded so they stood up on the plates. They'd come in, all apologetic, and I would say, "No problem. Look, I even fixed breakfast for us." I can't explain why I thought anyone would want breakfast in mid-afternoon. It made sense then. I must have been preoccupied, what with listening for their car to pull in, because

I made the pancakes all wrong so that they were runny and then I burned them.

I laughed some when I was cleaning up the mess I'd made, just knowing they'd come in right in the middle of it and tease me and tell me it was all right, and then we'd all go out for dinner. But it didn't happen that way. Finally, at about 8 P.M., I ended up eating cornflakes with warm milk and what was left of the thawed, soggy blueberries. I got my pillow and some blankets and made a bed for myself on the couch in front of the TV. That way they'd see me there when they came in. They'd be sorry and I'd be upset, but I would finally forgive them. I also didn't feel like going upstairs all by myself. Besides, Dad would pick me up and carry me to my room like he used to when I was a little girl. I knew I was much too big for that now, but the thought of it—of my dad's strong arms lifting me, my mom patting my face with her hand—calmed me down, and I went off to sleep.

When I woke up the next morning, on Monday, and found out I was still alone in the house, I guess

I should have called someone. But I didn't. I didn't get dressed for school. I didn't even turn off the TV, which had been going all night. I just sat and looked at the phone. The first time it rang, I jumped a mile. It was from work for Mom. I told them she was sick. I did the same thing when Dad's partner, Al Mondini, called from the bank to see where he was. Mom and I always call him Almond Al.

"Shouldn't you be at school, Molly?" Almond Al said.

"I should, but I'm sick, too," I said. I could hear the long pause at the other end of the line. If I was sick, he was wondering, how come I was talking on the phone now. So, just like my parents always said, one lie had to lead to another. "I'm better than they are, though," I said in a quick, nervous voice. "I mean, I didn't lose my voice like they did and so that is why I am answering the phone. But it hurts to talk, so I have to hang up now. Bye."

Maybe Almond Al was the one who got suspicious and called the police.

That night I went around to all the doors to

make sure they were still locked, and I checked the windows. I turned off the TV and then, because it seemed too quiet, I turned it on again. Not real loud, just on. I went upstairs and turned on the radio in Mom and Dad's bedroom, and I lay there for a while on top of their bed, listening to classical music. I still wasn't scared, but after a while I got up and went into my bedroom. I locked my door and put a chair in front of it. There's this song that Mom taught me once, one that she called a Lonesome Song, a song you sing when you're all alone and need a friend. If a friend hears you, they'll sing back to you.

I sang that Lonesome Song very softly to myself. "Hey yoo, hey yah neh . . ."

I kept on singing it. Even though no one answered, it made me feel less alone and I fell asleep.

The next morning was easier. I got up, got dressed, had more cornflakes, brushed my teeth, and caught the school bus at the bottom of our driveway. I didn't say anything to anyone about Mom and Dad being gone. They're on a trip, I was telling myself now. Everything is fine. They'll be back. I even remembered to make up a really official-looking note on my computer saying that I'd been sick and that was why I'd missed school, and I signed it with my mom's name. But maybe the way I worded it wasn't quite right. I know the woman in the office looked at me strangely when I handed it to her with a big smile. Maybe she was the one who made the call. Or maybe it was Ms. Shabbas. I smiled and laughed so much in class that day that Ms. Shabbas looked over at me with one eyebrow raised the way she always does when she thinks something is wrong. But I avoided talking with her. If I talked with her about it, then it would mean something was wrong.

I was so sure that everything would work out. I never doubted. Not even when the people came to the house the next night and started questioning me. Nor when the Social Services lady and the two cops escorted me out. I just kept saying, "I have to stay here. They'll be back." I even said that to the newspeople when they showed up. I don't know who called them. Maybe they just sensed it the way sharks smell blood and come swarming in when something has been wounded.

It just looks like I was crying on that TV show. The microphones make your voice sound all weird, like you are hysterical or something. And the lights make your eyes look all wild and scared. They even made mine water so much that you might have thought I was crying. I wasn't. I knew Mom and Dad would be back.

I still know they'll be back. But I don't want to talk about that. I just wanted to explain that I was never afraid. Not at all. Until later that night when this old guy showed up.

"Molly," the Social Services woman said, "someone is here for you, one of your relatives."

That was a big surprise to me. I didn't know I had any relatives anywhere near here. Mom is an orphan and all Dad's closest relatives are dead. It's a really sad story, how his brothers died in a car accident and his sister drowned, and then there was this big fire while Dad was away at school and his parents were in the house. That left only his two aunts to raise him, but they were old people and they died before I was born. I think that's the reason why we've never gone up to the reservation. There's nobody close to Dad there anymore, and that makes him too sad. But Dad had said that there were cousins and that maybe sometime we'd get to meet them, although they lived way out in California.

The Social Services woman led me into another room. A tall, elderly, thin man with stooped shoulders, all dressed in gray—even his shoes!—was standing there looking out the window.

"Here's your niece," the Social Services lady said in a chirpy voice. He turned around to look down at me with a face that was so thin it looked like bone. He didn't look Indian. Though his skin was almost as brown as my dad's, it was as if he'd dyed himself that color. His eyes were round and unblinking, like the eyes of an owl. He smiled, and I could see how big his teeth were.

"I don't know him," I said, taking a step backward.

"Of course not," chirped the lady. "He's been out

of the country." She smiled at him, and he nodded back at her. They were two adults, and I was just a kid. What could I know about anything? "You see," she said, taking the tone that certain grown-ups use with children and idiots—who are the same in their minds—"this is such a wonderful coincidence. Your great-uncle here moved into our town just two weeks ago without even knowing that your father, his own dear nephew, was here. He just happened to see the story on the news and came right over here. You are his flesh and blood, dear."

I looked up at him again, and he nodded. There was a little smile on his face. It was as if he knew what I was thinking, as if he knew I knew he wasn't who he said he was, but there was nothing I could do to stop this.

"I don't know him," I said again. "I've never heard of him. And I don't care if he *is* my uncle. My parents will be back soon. And my teacher said I could stay with her if you're worried about me being home by myself."

That was true. Ms. Shabbas had left only an hour

ago. She had come to the offices where I was being kept. She'd agreed with me that my parents would be back soon, but she had suggested that, just for now, I might like to stay with her, so I wouldn't have to be alone. But Social Services wouldn't hear of it. Not when an actual relative was coming to get me.

The lady shook her head. She was losing her patience. "Dear," she said, "we have checked things very thoroughly."

She turned and gestured to the tall stranger she was determined to hand me over to. The expression on her face said that she was sorry to bother him, but they needed to humor me to keep me from making a scene. He reached into his pocket and pulled out a big wallet. It was covered with snakeskin.

"Here," she said, taking the wallet and holding it out to me.

I put my hands behind my back. I didn't want to touch it.

"Oh!" she said in an exasperated voice. "Look!"

She flipped the wallet open. There was a driver's

license with a picture of the man who was saying he was my uncle. The picture looked more human than he did, but it was him. I looked over at him. A horrible thought came to me. Maybe I was the only one who could see him this way. Maybe he looked normal to other people. I snuck a glance at him. He gave me that little nod and knowing smile again. A shiver went down my back.

"Dea-arrr, look *here*," the lady said, her impatient finger pointing to the license. There was his name, the same last name as my family's. She flipped the license over to show me another clear plastic pocket with a photo in it. It was the smiling face of my father, the high school graduation photo he'd shown me more than once. She flipped again, and there was a picture of my dad and mom's wedding. The photos were just the same as those my dad always carried in his wallet. That wedding photo even seemed to have the same torn corner. . . .

She slapped the wallet shut and handed it back.

"Then it is settled," she said. "Until your parents return, you will be in the custody of your great-uncle."

And that was that. Unlike in a court of law, when grown-ups make a decision about a kid's future, there is no appeal.

I was just so worn-out from all the attention that I didn't protest. I let him take me to this old spooky house.

What was that? Footsteps, heavy ones on the stairs.

Now I am afraid.

THE KNOCK ON THE DOOR

I T'S THE SEVENTH NIGHT that I've been in this house. I should be ready for his routine by now, but I'm not. First there is the all too familiar sound of heavy feet thumping up the stairs: *thump, thump, thump.* Then there is a long silence while he catches his breath. *Thump, thump, thump* and silence. There are exactly thirty-six stairs, so he does this eleven times. The twelfth time is when I hear the wood on the landing creaking. Then comes the worst part. The silence. Because even though he makes noise coming up the stairs, the noise always stops when he reaches the top. Just that first creak when he steps up from the last stair.

And then nothing.

I imagine that his feet don't really move. He just glides half an inch above the rug, like Dracula in the movies. I know that can't be what happens. I know I'm just scaring myself and that it's the thickness of the rug in the hallway that cushions his steps so that I don't hear them. But even so, I find myself getting up from the bed to stand in the middle of the room, staring at the chair I have in front of the door. And I'm thinking, maybe, just maybe, he won't come to my door tonight. Maybe he'll just go down the hall and into his own room and hang by his toes from the rafters or whatever he does. Maybe he'll leave me in peace.

As always, I'm holding my breath. I'm listening like a deer does when it catches the scent of a mountain lion and then the wind changes so that it can't smell it anymore. But the deer knows the lion is out there somewhere. Maybe moving away, maybe getting closer, maybe . . .

WHACK-WHACK!

The crack of his bony knuckles against the thick wood of the door makes me jump a mile. But I don't scream, like I did the first night he did this after I was brought here.

"You all right?" he says. His voice isn't all that scary, even though it's muffled by the door and sounds as distant as the voice of a memory or a ghost.

I lean back away from the door, trying to make my voice sound as far away from it as possible.

"I'm okay. I'm in bed. I'm going to sleep," I say. Then I wait.

SNICK! That's it. It's the sound of the lock on the outside. Like every other night, he's locked me in. The first night it scared me, but now it makes me breathe a sigh of relief. I count out under my breath. One, two, three, four, five, six. And then I hear it. The sound of his feet going back down the stairs. And unless he comes floating down the halls at midnight, or maybe flying outside to peer in my windows, that's it for the night. I can try to go to sleep now. I'm locked in and, I guess, safe.

And, like the other nights before this, I will try not to think about what it is that I am locked in against. I'll try not to think about why there are bars on my windows.

I look around the room. There's not much to see. There's the four-poster bed, the bedside stand, and a table by the window, which is covered with thick purple curtains. The walls are bare, though there are square- and rectangular-shaped places where the wood isn't quite so dark. I guess there used to be pictures hanging there. There's no closet, just one of those old stand-up wardrobes. It has only six coat hangers in it, but my stuff is still in the suitcase and the cardboard box I brought with me. I'm not planning on staying long, so I don't want to unpack. All the furniture in the room seems to be pretty old, all made of dark wood. The rug on the floor is new and it is cream colored. It doesn't really go with everything else in the room, but at least it means that things aren't so dark in here. I'm grateful for that because the only light is the one on the nightstand and it's got a 40-watt bulb in it. There's also a light in the bathroom, which is attached to the room. I always leave the bathroom door open with the light turned on.

I walk over to the window. Bad idea, a voice is saying to me. But I'm doing it anyway. Don't look outside. But I can't help myself. I reach for the curtain, feel the heavy fabric in my hand, pull it back.

The whole world explodes in a great burst of light and sound.

THE DREAM

I DON'T SCREAM. IT was only thunder and lightning, a rumble that shook the whole building as if it were a dollhouse rocked by a giant's heavy foot thudding down next to it. When there was lightning Mom always said it was the flashbulb of the Creator taking pictures with a giant camera.

Dad always said thunder is the rumbling steps of the Henos, the Thunder Beings, who live in the sky. They're good guys who throw down lightning like spears to destroy monsters.

But this time, at least, their lightning spears seem to have missed. In that moment of absolute brightness outside, my eyes took their own quick picture, one that made me yank the curtains back in place and get into bed with the covers over my head. What had I seen in the flash of lightning? Down there, on the lawn, his face shaded by a wide-brimmed hat, was a man. A tall man, skinny as a skeleton. He was standing at the door of an old shed. It was my uncle.

My mind is going a million miles a minute now. Why was he there? What is he doing? Am I just being paranoid or am I really in some kind of danger? My mind keeps going back to that shed, too. It's a lot older and bigger than the little plywood one Dad has in back of our house. It doesn't have any windows in it like Dad's shed, just one heavy door with a new padlock on it. What was my uncle going to do in that shed in the middle of the night?

I can't find an answer. So I turn it all off by thinking of Ms. Showbiz singing. I think of her singing that song from the musical about Annie, another orphan—assuming I might be one, which I know I really am not. "Tomorrow, tomorrow . . ." And as I put all my thoughts and fears into imagining her singing, I fall asleep. And I dream.

It's like some of the dreams I've had before. I know I am dreaming, but I can't wake up. It is what my dad calls an "aware dream." That is a dream where you know you are a dreamer and, if you are alert enough, you'll get some help from your dream. Someone or something will guide you or give you a message. But I am too busy running to look for a guide. Whatever is chasing me is getting closer. I can feel its hot breath on the back of my neck and I know its bony hands are about to grab me.

Then the dream changes. I am in a cave. I live in that cave and I am not alone there. Someone is sitting in the corner of the cave, his face turned away from me. "Hold out your arm, child!" he says in a rough voice. I hold my arm out toward him, and he reaches back to feel it without looking around. His long, dry fingers squeeze my forearm. "Thin as a stick, thin as a stick," he growls. "Go into the forest and check your snares. You must eat more, my niece. Eat and grow fat."

In an eyeblink I'm not in the cave but in the forest. I'm dressed in deerskin, checking the snares I've placed on the trails. I'm worried because I haven't caught anything. My uncle will be angry.

Then I see motion in the brush. Something is struggling at the side of the path. It's a rabbit, its hind foot caught in one of my snares. I lift my stick to hit it. But the rabbit looks up at me and speaks.

"Little Sister," the rabbit says, "spare my life, and I will help you save your own life."

I put down my stick and loosen the cord from the rabbit's foot. It doesn't run away when it is free. Instead it looks me in the eye and speaks again.

"Little Sister," the rabbit says, "thank you for sparing me. Now I will tell you what you must know. The one you think is your uncle is not human."

DARK CEDARS

I CAN STILL HEAR the rabbit's voice when I open
my eyes. I look at the clock next to my bed. It
is morning, time to get ready for school. I rum-
mage through my suitcase and the cardboard box
and find what I need. I don't feel like putting my
clothes into the creepy wardrobe. When I was little
my mom read me that book about the wardrobe
and the lion and the witch. I wished then that I had
a magic wardrobe that I could crawl into and end

up in some strange land. Now that I really am in a strange land all I want to do is crawl back home. But if there was some kind of magic door in that wardrobe, it'd probably take me someplace even worse than this.

I take my toothbrush and go into the bathroom. The only good thing about the room is that it has a bathroom connected to it. It means I don't have to go out into the hall or downstairs yet and see him. There's a bathroom built in because the former owners tried to run a bed and breakfast. There's actually an old sign leaning on its side against the house: DARK CEDARS BED AND BREAKFAST. The name alone is enough to scare people away from it. But I think it probably just didn't work out because this place is too far from the center of town, even though it is near Three Falls Gorge, which is the town's main place of "scenic beauty," as our chamber of commerce puts it. When my uncle got this place he took down the sign.

While I am in the bathroom I look at myself in the small, smoky mirror hanging over the sink. I think I have the kind of face that only a mother could love, but both my parents tell me I'm wrong. They think thick eyebrows that almost meet in the middle and ink–black hair that grows so thick I need hedge clippers to trim it are positive assets. "There's so much you can do with that hair," my mother says. Like get it cut short and dyed blond. My nose is okay, not bumpy or too short or too long, but my lips are too thick. My cheeks look as if I have apples stuffed in them, and when I smile my teeth are straight, but there is this gap between my incisors on top. "Braces will do wonders for you, dear." As if, I think. I can't wait until I'm old enough to get a real makeover like they have sometimes on the shopping channel.

Still, though I'm not thrilled with how I look, I don't hate my looks. I can just see lots of room for improvement. And I know that people must like my face at least a little because whenever I smile at someone they almost always smile back. Except for my uncle. I tried smiling at him yesterday. He just studied my face like a scientist looking at some strange new bug until my smile crawled away and died. I won't try that again.

I sigh and lift up my chin. At least I don't look like a terrified victim in some slasher movie. I just look like a kid about to catch the bus. I leave the bathroom and try the door. It's not locked from the outside anymore. It never is by this time. I peek outside carefully, my backpack with a large, empty plastic container in it over my shoulder. No sign of anyone up or down the hall.

As soon as I start down the creaky stairs, he hears me.

"Come down to breakfast," he whispers up the stairs. He's standing at the bottom, half hidden by the old coatrack. He turns and walks away. He doesn't like me to see his face in the morning. Or ever, for that matter.

I go into the sunroom. It looks like it used to be a screened porch once. It has a floor of cold stone tiles and is connected to the back of the house. Its four big windows and sliding glass door were probably meant to let in the sun and give you a view of the garden. But there is no sun today, and there hasn't been a garden out there for a while. The places where flowers once grew are overgrown with nettles and burdock and a few small sumac trees, their leaves all red now that there's been a frost.

Although there's room in the sunroom for several tables, there's just the one. It's a glass-topped table with rusty blue metal legs. The two chairs are made of that same rusty blue metal with curlicue designs. The table is set for one. As always, he's already eaten. At least that's what he says. I've never seen evidence of his breakfast. I see his back as he goes out the sunroom door. I'm never allowed to go out that way toward the big shed in the backyard with heavy-duty hinges on the thick, bolted doors. His toolroom, he says. I wonder again what he was doing out there last night.

"Eat your breakfast," he calls back without turning his head. "You're looking thin."

Then he's gone, and I take my first real breath of the day. The food on the table looks good. I'm hungry. Grapefruit, cereal, toast with butter and jam. I put my backpack under the table between my knees. I take the lid off the plastic container in the backpack and pretend to eat. But each spoonful of cereal, each slice of toast, each piece of fruit goes into the plastic box. I snap the lid onto it and close the backpack. Then I pretend to wipe my lips with the paper napkin, ball it up, and put it on the now empty plate.

I'm just in time because, just as he's done every other day, he sticks his head out of the door of the shed to see if I've eaten my food.

"Done," I call out in a cheery voice. Then I stand up and walk to the front door, trying to be as calm as possible, hoping that it will not be locked. It isn't, and I escape down the walk to the corner where the school bus will arrive within five minutes. Time enough to dump the food down the storm drain at the curb edge. Let the rats deal with it.

Super paranoid, that is what you are saying now. Melodramatic. But I'm determined not to eat the food he gives me. I think he puts something into it. When I first got here I ate what he put in front of me automatically. I started having a headache and my heart was racing, and I felt like some kind of zombie. When I went to bed that night I just conked out. I didn't even dream. The next day I started my Tupperware routine. If I'd kept eating that food I'd probably be walking with my arms held out in front of me saying, "Yes, Master!" in a hollow voice whenever he spoke to me.

When the bus comes I take the first seat. Other kids are sitting with friends, but I stay by myself. This isn't the bus I used to take. No one in my class is on it, and people are still checking me out. I haven't been in a hurry to be all bright and cheery with my new busmates, either.

When the bus stops in front of the school, though, I have to start smiling. This is my place of refuge. I'm safe here. Other kids might groan when they walk through the big front doors, but I breathe a sigh of relief. It's all so routine and boring here. I love it. Although when Laura Loh, who is my second-best friend, waves to me from her locker, I pretend not to see her and just go straight into class. I know she wants to talk to me about Greg Iverson and how cute he is and do I think he likes her . . . and I can't bear it. For some reason I just can't think of anything to say to other kids right now, and all the stuff that used to interest me seems kind of unreal.

In our class it is Don Quixote Day. At least it is for Ms. Showbiz. We are all groaning by the time she finishes belting out her medley from *Man of La Mancha*. I'm groaning the loudest of all because it just makes me feel so safe, so . . . normal. I feel so great that when Ms. Shabbas tells us to open our workbooks, I burst out in laughter that is so loud and inappropriate that everyone, including Ms. Shabbas, looks at me. Maureen Viola, who is my best friend and who sits two seats away, looks at me and mouths the words: "What is wrong with you?"

All of a sudden I feel as if I am about to burst into tears. I have to put my head down on my desk. What *is* wrong with me? I'm not being tortured or anything. My uncle was kind enough to take me in. He's just a little strange. Maybe I'm the truly strange one with my worries about being drugged and my blockading my door at night and imagining what might be happening in that shed. Too much imagination, that's me.

Ms. Shabbas has a little talk with me that afternoon. She asks me to wait behind when the rest of the class is leaving for gym. She's worried about my behavior. "Is everything all right," she pauses, ". . . at home?"

What home? That is what I want to say. I want to scream and cry and have her hold me in her arms while I sob against her shoulder. But what good would that do? So I give her my patented sunny smile.

"Everything is fine," I say. "Really fine."

But Ms. Shabbas doesn't smile back. "Really?" she says in a soft voice. Then she looks beyond that smile, right into my eyes as if she can see my thoughts. It's not the way my uncle does it, not like someone stealing a part of me. It's not even like an adult looking at a kid who's being unreasonable. It's the way a true friend looks at you when they say they want to help you and really mean it.

"No," I whisper. "It's not."

And then I tell her. I don't tell her everything because now that I'm in school, my fears seem a little foolish, and I don't want her to think I'm being melodramatic. But I tell her how I feel, how weird it is in my uncle's house, how I really, really don't want to be there. She doesn't interrupt or ask questions.

She just listens, nodding every now and then. When I'm done I feel lighter, as if I'm no longer carrying a ten-ton truck on my shoulders.

Ms. Shabbas lightly places her hands on my shoulders. She doesn't say I'm being foolish or that I should grow up.

"Sweetheart," she says. "Thank you for telling me." She turns slightly to write something on a card that she hands to me. "Here's my home phone and my cell phone. Call me anytime. Okay? We'll keep an eye on this together, right?"

"Right," I say. And for the rest of the day in school things almost do seem right.

But then I take one more deep breath and the school day is over. That's bad. The only good thing is that it is Wednesday. That means I get to come back to school tomorrow and the next day before the weekend comes, which most kids love because it means we won't have to go back to school for two days. Two whole days.

I walk home because it takes longer than the bus. I stop at a fast-food place to eat enough to kill my appetite. I don't have much money left, and I don't know what I'll do when it runs out. But I try not to worry about that now. There are other, more pressing concerns.

Finally it is getting dark. I can't avoid it anymore. I'm headed back to the house of doom.

EAT AND GROW FAT

YOU MAY BE ASKING yourself what life is like for me inside that house. Are there spiderwebs everywhere? Bats and centipedes and mold on the walls? Are there chains clanking down in the cellar and ghostly moans coming from the attic?

No. Actually, aside from being dark and set back from the road, it isn't really all that spooky a place to look at. It's a hundred years old, but there are older places in town. And the house is full of modern appliances in the kitchen and the living room. Dishwasher, microwave, a television with a cable hookup. My uncle even has a personal computer. I saw it through the open door of his study once. He spends a lot of his time in that room and I imagine he must be surfing the Net, visiting all the weirdest websites, probably.

What makes that house strange is the way it feels when you get inside it. I saw an old movie once where someone walks into a room and then the door disappears and the walls start moving in. It is something like that. And I always feel as if someone or something is looking at me, but when I turn around there's nothing there.

Then there's the way my uncle acts. Like when you'd expect him to be waiting for me, his niece, to come home, and to ask me how my day went, he's not. He's not here. There's just a note on the front door, not handwritten, but out of his laser printer. "Back later," it reads. "Dinner in fridge."

He's left food for me in the refrigerator for the last two nights as well. The food I'm supposed to eat is on a plate on the top shelf, ready to pop into the microwave. Anyhow, it makes it easier for me. I flip on the garbage disposal and spoon the loathsome stuff, a huge plate of spaghetti with meatballs, down the sink drain. If I ate everything he gave me—even if it wasn't full of drugs—I'd get as fat as a butterball turkey.

I could go into the living room and watch TV. Or one of the videos from the library of movies he has next to the VCR. There's a lot of stuff that some people think kids like to watch. Mostly Disney movies and cartoons. But I don't want to. It's the thought of having him walk in while I'm watching something. Or, even worse, of him watching me without my knowing it. I've got homework and books to read in my backpack. I'm seeing more of the school librarian now than I ever did before my parents turned up missing. Before I go upstairs I look out the kitchen window and see that the light is on in front of his shed. That either means he is out there or he forgot to turn it off. No way am I going out there to find out which it is.

I put the chair in front of my door and then take

a quick bath, put on my pjs and my favorite pink robe, which I have worn just about every night for a year now. I move the bedside lamp closer so I can get the most out of its feeble light, lie down on my stomach, and breeze through my homework. Even the math problems are really no problem at all. Then I pull out one of the books I've borrowed. It's one that Ms. Shabbas once said I just had to read because you can really identify with the heroine and it takes you somewhere else. Which is where I want to be, for sure.

It turns out that she was right. The book truly does take my mind off things. Before I know it I've read a dozen chapters. I feel like I'm on a sailing ship with the heroine. Until I start wondering what Charlotte Doyle would do if she switched places with me. And I realize that I don't know what she would do any more than I know what I should do. I put a bookmark in to keep my place, lean back on my pillow, and close my eyes. As always, at least since I've been here, I don't turn out the light. I just want to rest my eyes. I don't want to go to sleep.

But I do.

And, instantly, I am there in that same dream. I'm back in the cave, the body of a partridge warm and limp in my hands. I'm holding it out to my uncle as he crouches in his corner. Without looking over his shoulder, he reaches an arm back. I see for the first time that his fingers are long and hairy and his fingernails are thick and sharp, more like claws. He grabs the dead bird so hard that I hear its bones crack.

"I thought it would be a rabbit," he growls. "Did you catch a rabbit?"

"No," I say. "This is all."

Then he begins to eat. I don't see him eat it, but I hear his teeth crunching through feathers and flesh and bones. He eats it all, growling as he swallows.

Then he reaches his arm back again. I stare at his fingers. A few small feathers from the partridge are stuck to them and the nails are red with blood.

"Hold out your arm, child," he says.

I don't give him my arm. Instead I hold out a stick the size of my wrist. His groping hand closes about it.

"Arrggh," he growls. "Even thinner and harder

than before. No flesh at all, only bone. You must eat more, my niece. Eat and grow fat for me."

I sit up. I'm awake.

I say that aloud. "I'm awake. It was all a dream."

But then I look around me and I see this room—as bare and cold as the chamber of a cave. And then the *snick, snick, snick* of the locks.

No, it wasn't a dream.

NO PICTURES

THERE ARE NO PHOTOS at all in this house. No pictures of any kind, no paintings, not even any mirrors, aside from that small cloudy one in my bathroom. Even that was not up on the wall at first. I found it tucked behind the wardrobe and hung it up in the bathroom. Whenever I leave each day I take it off the bathroom wall and carefully put it in its original hiding place. I just have this feeling that if I don't do that, it will be gone when I come back. There is nothing else in this house to show his face or anyone else's.

When he picked me up, he smiled and laughed and talked like a concerned adult. It must have been an effort for him. His face was drawn and thin, angular with high cheekbones and a chin that jutted out, a high forehead with only a fringe of hair around his ears. But he looked human then.

As soon as he got me into the car, he started to change. I remember him putting on sunglasses and pulling his big hat down so that his face was concealed from me and from other drivers. I caught a glimpse of the side of his face every now and then, and it seemed as if the flesh was melting off his bones. At the time I figured the light was playing tricks on me, but now I'm not so sure. Ever since that day he's been careful not to show me his face at all. He always keeps his back to me.

And his hands! He'd kept them in his pockets, hidden from the Social Services people. But I could see them as they held the wheel. They were white, pale, pale white. And the skin on them was so thin that I thought I could see through to the bones.

And the fingernails were thick and long and sharp like claws. He must have seen me looking because he slipped on a pair of leather gloves at the next stoplight. Then I turned away to watch the trees and telephone poles and the houses whizzing past, being left behind us as we went down that road toward someplace I never wanted to go.

He didn't speak much that day. He just opened the car door when we got to the house.

"Get out," he whispered.

I got out.

"Go in," he said.

I went in.

"Eat."

I ate the plate of food he put in front of me while he stood behind me and watched until I was done.

"Your room is upstairs," he said.

And I went up to it with my box and my suitcase, and he shut the door behind me and locked it. I remember wondering that night if the door would ever be unlocked again. I also remember not caring whether I lived or died. I missed my parents so much. And then I remember feeling zombielike and conking out.

I still miss them. But I can't believe that they're gone forever. Dad always told me that being a dreamer meant that I had a special kind of gift like our old people had long ago. If they really were never going to come back I'd know somehow through my dreams. But I haven't had that kind of dream. Instead, I just have this feeling that they're out there somewhere and that they will be back. And when they come back I will be there and they'll hug me and explain why they were gone and things will be all right again. I do care whether I live or die.

It is the middle of the night. It is still Wednesday night, a night that just doesn't seem to want to end, that just keeps creeping along. But my mind is moving like a runaway freight train. Run away, that's exactly what I feel like doing. But run away where? First of all I've got almost no money, and without it I wouldn't get far. He'd find me and bring me right back here.

But that is not the only reason I haven't run away. I have this feeling that if I'm ever going to see my mother and father again, I need to be here. That somehow my uncle is involved in their disappearance, even though he didn't show up until after they were gone.

Trust your dreams. Both my parents said that. That's our old way, our Mohawk way. The way of our ancestors. Trust the little voice that speaks to you. That is your heart speaking. But when those feelings, those dreams, those voices are so confusing, what do you do then?

"Help," I whisper. "Help."

I'm not sure who I'm talking to when I say that, but I hope they're listening.

THE COUNSELOR

WHEN THE MORNING COMES I haven't dreamed again. I haven't slept. I've been thinking about what I can do, and I've made up my mind. I've got a plan at last. It's a simple one, but simple ones are probably the best. It's also the only thing I can think to do.

At school you are always hearing about kids with problems. And there are people called counselors whose job is supposed to be to help kids who have them. It seems to me that most kids never actually see them. At our school, at least, the counselor is kept busy by the kids who are always in trouble or getting into trouble. Her name is Mrs. Rudder. Unless you are frothing at the mouth or something, it just isn't easy to get in to her.

As soon as I walk into the classroom I go right up to Ms. Shabbas. She doesn't do the adult thing of seeming to listen while not really hearing you because she thinks she already has the answer. She listens so well that she even forgets to sing whatever show tune she's picked out for that morning.

"It's gotten worse for me," I tell her. "It's driving me crazy. Every night when I hear him lock me in my room I think I'm going to scream."

Ms. Shabbas sits up straighter at that. "He locks you in? You didn't tell me about that before."

As soon as class goes out to rec, she takes me straight to the counselor's office. The door is partially open. I've walked by the door a million times and never gone in before. Ms. Shabbas pushes it open the rest of the way and pulls me in with her.

One whole wall to the left of the desk is taken up with pigeonholes. Not the kind that you put mail in, but smaller. Every one has the name of a kid written under it, and in every pigeonhole is a little pill bottle. Ritalin and stuff like that. The kids who need meds have to take their daily pill in Mrs. Rudder's office. There's a water cooler and paper cups, lots of them. On the other wall are some posters about not smoking and not taking drugs. I guess the two walls balance each other out.

"Can I help you?" says a voice from behind us that sounds like the person mostly wants to help us to leave.

We turn around and Mrs. Rudder is standing there. She's not very tall, but she has this way of looking at people that makes them feel as if they're being shrunk down under a microscope.

Ms. Shabbas, though, refuses to be diminished.

"Molly needs to talk to someone."

"I can make an appointment for . . ." Mrs. Rudder says, stepping past us to her desk and starting to look at her appointment book.

"Now!" Ms. Shabbas says.

"I'm very busy," Mrs. Rudder replies. "I'm sure this can—"

"This child is afraid," Ms. Shabbas says. "Look at her eyes." She won't take no for an answer.

The next thing I know, I'm sitting in the chair and Mrs. Rudder is leaning over her desk asking me questions and taking notes while Ms. Shabbas listens.

At first I can't make any headway. I'm telling the truth, but I feel like I'm not giving the right answers to the questions I am asked in a calm, matter-of-fact way.

"Has he ever touched you in a bad way?"

"No."

"Hmmm." Mrs. Rudder nods. "So he's never hit you?"

"No."

"Has he ever threatened you?"

"Not really."

"Ah-hah," Mrs. Rudder says. She looks over at Ms. Shabbas and shakes her head. I can tell that she thinks I am wasting her time. She's no longer sitting but standing up in a way that makes me feel as if I'll be standing up soon, on my way out her door. "What has he done that makes you afraid?"

I know what I want to say. I want to say that I see him looking at me out of the corner of his eye in a way that makes chills go down my back. Even when I'm walking down the hall and going into my room I feel like I'm still being looked at. It is as if eyes are watching me wherever I go in his house. I want to tell her that whenever he comes into a room, the air gets colder. Whenever I know he is thinking about me I have that feeling like someone is walking over my grave. I want to say that he's not really a human being, he is something else. I don't know what. He is fattening me up. But if I say that, they'll suspect I'm nuts. I want to tell them about my dreams. But I know that if I tell Mrs. Rudder my dreams are warning me about the danger I'm in, she'll move from mere suspicion to absolute certainty that I'm lying.

Instead, I say the one thing that does get her attention.

"He locks me in my room at night."

Mrs. Rudder sits back down. She looks right at me over her desk, her hands clutched together. "Every night?"

"Every night."

"Can you come out if you ask?"

"I don't think so."

More things are said, but this was a big one. I see Ms. Shabbas nodding to me. Mrs. Rudder has listened. She'll do something.

But not much.

That afternoon Mrs. Rudder and a man who is introduced to me as Mr. Wintergreen from Child Welfare escort me to the house. Ms. Shabbas wanted to come along, but Mrs. Rudder told her that it wouldn't be following proper procedure.

He's waiting because they've called him on the phone an hour before we get there. Plenty of time for him to get ready. He's wearing his hat and a human face again and he smiles at them. They don't seem to notice that he doesn't offer to shake hands, that he keeps his hands in the pockets of his sweater.

"Your niece is very upset," Mrs. Rudder says to him.

"I understand," he says. "She's had a lot to deal with."

They follow him upstairs. He shows them the door to my room. There is no lock on the outside of the door. Never was. And no sign of screw holes that would be there if a lock had been removed. The only lock is on the inside. See, there's the release for the lock on the inside of the door, he tells them. Her side of the door. She can get out any time she wants.

"She's a very imaginative child," he adds.

I can't say anything. How can I say that he had time enough to change the door frame and the door? It wouldn't make any difference no matter what I said. They believe him, not me. I'm the melodramatic one. He's just a kindly older man who's taken in a difficult young relative.

They stand up. They're going to go and leave me there with him.

Mrs. Rudder leans over and places a hand on my shoulder. "Molly, dear," she says. "If you are still having these anxiety attacks, I can fit you into my calendar next week."

She looks up at my uncle and smiles. "Thank you for your time."

I hold my hand up as they walk toward the door as if to stop them. I want to scream, but I can't. They think I'm waving and they wave back to me as they go through the door, as it closes behind them, as my uncle goes over to the door and locks it.

As he turns, without looking at me, I wonder what he is going to say, what he is going to do . . .

But he doesn't say anything about it. It's as if he has no anger, no real emotions at all.

"Your dinner is in the refrigerator" is all he says. Then he goes upstairs. I can hear the whirring of an electric screwdriver. I don't even have to guess what he's doing. After a while he comes down and walks out the back door to his work shed.

That night, when I am in my room and my door is closed, I hear his feet coming up the stairs. Then, after that moment of heart-stopping silence, there is the familiar sound. *Snick*. As he locks my door from the outside.

THE GIRL IN THE STORY

It's worse than it was before. Now he knows how I really feel about him. He knows that I suspect him. That means he'll be twice as watchful.

To calm myself, I try to imagine him sitting in front of his computer or out in his toolshed, a normal person doing normal things. But I can't. All I can see in my mind is the image of the cave creature from my dream crouched in the corner, its long, uncombed hair over its face, its clawed hand reaching backward to grasp my arm to see if I am fat enough to eat. I don't want to think about that.

I stretch out on the bed. It is all so hopeless. I try to remember one of the funny stories that Dad tells, ones in which the things that happen are so silly you just have to laugh. Some of them are old stories, but some are about things that happened to him when he was a kid, like the time when he talked his little brother into jumping into a muddy pond with all his clothes on to try to catch a turtle. Then, realizing his little brother was going to get into trouble because he'd gotten his clothes dirty, Dad jumped in, too, so that both of them would be in trouble. That way the trouble would be only half as bad for each of them, Dad explained. Maybe that doesn't sound funny to you, but the way Dad told it always made me laugh. Thinking about it I almost do laugh, until another thought comes to me. I may never hear my father's voice again. Then the little smile that had started to form on my face disappears.

I'm so sure that I won't be able to sleep that it surprises me when I realize I'm dreaming again. I am no longer in the room that has never been mine. Instead I am standing in a forest. I know I haven't gotten there by sleepwalking. Even if the door had been left unlocked and I'd found my way out of the house, I could never have found a place like this in the waking world. The trees are so big, bigger than the redwoods of California that I've seen in pictures. There haven't been trees that big around here in central New York for three hundred years or more.

The trees are not the only clue that I'm somewhere other than the usual waking world. The two figures who stand in front of me make it more than clear that I'm back in that dream. One of them is the same rabbit I saw before. It's a snowshoe rabbit. It wears its summer coat of brown, not the white of winter that it puts on when the snow is on the ground. It's more than twice as big as the little cottontail rabbits that I sometimes see at the edge of the school playground by the little patch of woods.

The other one is me. How strange to be me, looking at me. I blink twice at that. But there are subtle differences. The other me has skin that is a little more tanned than mine. Her hair is longer,

61

and there is a little scar on her cheek, just below her left eye, as if something sharp—a knife or a claw—cut across it once. She is also dressed the way I remember being dressed in my dream of the cave. Moccasins, deerskin dress, braided rawhide bracelet on her wrist. I stare at that bracelet. I remember my mother telling me about bracelets like that that Mohawk children used to wear to make sure they woke up safely from their dreams.

I blink my eyes again and the other me is gone. Or is she? I'm standing next to the rabbit now. There are moccasins on my feet, there's a rawhide brace-let around my wrist, and I'm wearing her deerskin dress . . . my deerskin dress.

"I'm in someone else's story," I blurt out.

"No, Little Sister," says a kind voice at my feet. "It is not someone else's story."

I look down at the rabbit. "What?" I say.

"This is your story now," the rabbit continues. "But even though it is your story, you are not safe. You must be brave. Your spirit must still remain strong."

For some reason, that makes me angry. After all that's happened I don't need some furry Oprah Winfrey to tell me I need to get my spiritual act in order.

"Is that all you've got to say?" I ask the rabbit, clenching my fists. "That I'm in trouble? Don't you think I know that?"

The rabbit hops close to me and places its front paws on my feet as it looks up at me.

"Little Sister," it says, "I am here to tell you something."

"What?" I ask in a voice that is no longer angry, a voice that is small and halting.

"Your parents," the rabbit says, "they have been buried."

"No," I whisper. "They can't be dead." I want to shout, but to do that I'd have to catch my breath, and right now it feels as if I can't breathe at all.

The rabbit's paws are patting my knee.

"Little Sister," the rabbit says, "I did not say they were dead. If they were dead, then you could not help them. They are buried but not dead."

Buried but not dead? Can I find hope in that? And if I can't understand what it means, how can I help them? I'm confused and I want to ask the rabbit to explain, but before I can do so it is gone.

I sit up, looking around for the rabbit, reaching for it . . . and I find myself grasping the blankets of my bed.

PICTURES

I WAS INTERVIEWED TODAY by a bunch of people. The nurse, the school psychologist, Mrs. Rudder. They think my problem may be a chemical one and that I need counseling. They think that my story about my uncle was brought on by the stress of uncertainty combined with my already imaginative personality. Lucky I didn't tell them about the rabbit dream.

Ms. Shabbas talks with me after school about it all.

"If you ask me, witch doctors know more about people than some of these professionals," she says. "If there's a problem, throw a prescription at it. That's all they seem to know lately."

I wonder why she is talking to me this way. I don't think most teachers would. But Ms. Shabbas is not most teachers. When she likes someone, trusts someone, she really talks to them. I've never realized before how much she likes me.

"Honey," she says, "I don't care if they didn't find any lock on your door. My bones tell me something's rotten in the state of Denmark. We got trouble right here in River City. *Comprende?*"

I nod. Part of me wants to jump up and down, pump my fist into the air, and yell, "Yes!" But even though I have an ally now, there may not be much she can do. Plus I'm still sick—and confused—about what I heard in my dream, those words the rabbit said. My parents are buried.

"Listen," Ms. Shabbas whispers, breaking into my thoughts. "I'm not saying do anything stupid. But bring me something solid to make your case, I'll move heaven and earth to get you away from that man. Just be careful, hear me?"

"I will," I say. But I am also thinking that it may not matter whether I am careful or not. Tomorrow is Friday. Whenever I think of that, I start feeling even more scared.

I'm the last one to get onto the bus. The driver's not happy that he had to wait for me, but Ms. Shabbas called down and told him to hold on till I got there. A truck pulls up behind the bus as I get on. Men climb out carrying toolboxes and equipment like drills, power saws, big wrenches, and cable cutters. The school is being hooked up to the information superhighway. They'll be here again tomorrow, then finish after the weekend. The weekend that begins tomorrow afternoon.

By the time I get to the house, I am just about overcome by a feeling of dread. It doesn't help that the days are getting much shorter now and it is almost dark already. As I open the door and go inside, a little shiver goes down my spine.

"Hello," I call. No one answers. I look into the kitchen. No note telling me to eat. I wonder if something is wrong, something more wrong than usual, I should say. I walk back into the hall and I notice that the door to my uncle's study is open. It is rarely open and it draws me, like a moth to a flame. Step by step I walk down the hall. I'm trying to stop myself, but I can't. The only thing I seem to be able to do is go more slowly so that my steps don't make the floor creak like it would if I went faster. I try to walk the way my father taught me that our Mohawk ancestors would when they wanted to go through the forest without making any noise. My elbows close to my sides, my hands held in front of me, I place one foot down slowly, then another, until I reach the study door.

It's a small room. My uncle isn't in there; there's no place he could hide. His chair is pushed back from the desk as if he suddenly had to go somewhere. I can see, though, the one window at the back of the room out into the yard. The toolshed door is open and a light is coming out of it. That must be it. For some reason he had to get up and go out to the shed to do something.

I should turn around now. I should not go into that room. But I still do.

There's a color laser printer next to the computer, the kind that does really high-quality prints on heavy glossy paper. Just like regular photographs. But what attracts my attention are the three small TV monitors on the shelf above the computer. I take another step closer and I freeze.

I feel as if I have been kicked in the stomach. I'm unable to move. My mouth is open and I think I'm about to scream. But I don't. Instead I will myself to thaw out, tell my feet to start moving me out of that room before my uncle comes back. I get up the stairs. I'm just opening the door to my room when I hear the front door open.

"Where are you?" my uncle calls. His raspy voice is a little out of breath, maybe a little worried. "Where are you?" he calls again, louder this time.

"Up here," I call back. "I don't feel good. I'm going to bed."

His heavy feet are coming up the stairs faster than usual. I shut the door before he gets to me.

He's breathing hard, waiting outside in the hall. He doesn't speak and neither do I. Finally, he snicks the lock and goes back downstairs. I crouch in the corner of the room with my arms around my legs. All I can see, even when I close my eyes, are the pictures on those TV screens. Live pictures from the hidden cameras trained on the front door, the back door, and the door to my room.

10

LOOKING

EVEN THOUGH I'M MORE afraid than I've ever been, I'm thinking fast as I crouch in the corner curled into a ball, hoping I'm out of sight of the cameras. I have so many questions in my mind. When did he set up those TV cameras and why haven't I seen them? Why does he have them set up like that? Then there is the scariest question of all. What will he do next?

I've got to be logical, though. That is what Mom

always tells me. Think first before you try to run away from a problem, otherwise you might run right into an even worse one. And stay alert.

I've always been a light sleeper. Dad used to say it was because I had warrior genes and he'd tease me about it, calling me Warrior Girl. He told me my Indian name might be Keeps Herself Awake. In the old days I would have been the one told to keep watch at night against enemies. Neither he nor Mom could ever come into my room at night without my waking up instantly.

There is no way that my so-called uncle can sneak into my room without my knowing it. Unless I've been drugged. But I haven't felt strange since that first night. I've stayed away from the food. I'm certain now that the person who calls himself my uncle is an impostor at best, and something much more terrible at worst. I begin to think of my dream, of the similarities between the creature fattening up the girl and my uncle. Skeleton Man. He's a modern-day Skeleton Man and this house is his cave. A glimmer of hope appears to me. If it really is like my dream, maybe I can find an answer in my dreams about what to do.

It is too cold in the corner and it's hard to think there. I get up and climb on the bed and let my head fall back onto the pillow. I start remembering back to the times I've come awake in the night since I've been here. Lots of times, now that I think of it. And every time it's been because I've had the feeling that I've been watched. I've just opened one eye, slowly, just a little. Not enough for anyone to notice I'm no longer sleeping. My whole body has been awake and waiting to act each time I've done this. But I've never seen anything. There has never been anyone else in my room. Never. But maybe there's a TV camera set up to look at me in here, too. Maybe the monitor for that camera is in his bedroom down the hall.

I look up at the ceiling. Up there is where it must be. We've learned about fiber optics in school and I know just how small the opening can be for a lens. No more than a pinhole. There's a light fixture right over my head. I'm betting that is where it is. If I piled my suitcase and my box on my bed and climbed up on top of them, I could probably reach it. The ceiling is only about eight feet high. But I won't do that now. I don't want him to know that I know. This has to be like a chess match. Never let your opponent know what your next move will be until you make it.

I think of what Dad taught me about chess. He loves the game and is always coaxing me to play it with him. Chess is a game based on war, on two armies starting out equal and trying to wipe each other out. Not with brute force, but with strategy, with thinking ahead much farther than one move.

My so-called uncle probably doesn't think of this as chess or any kind of an equal contest. He probably thinks that he has all the weapons. He's just playing with me.

But if I think of this as a chess game, it gives me an advantage. I can't just be a victim. I have to counter, even find some way to attack. Great, I think. But now what will my move be? I know that I have to make one. And it has to be a good one. Something my dad said comes back to me, some of the Mohawk warrior wisdom he was always teaching me. "It doesn't matter if you are the hunted or the hunter. Sometimes the most important thing you can do in a tough situation is to keep quiet, breathe slowly, and think."

So that is what I do—sit quietly for a long time. Finally, I think I know what to do.

First of all, I don't take off my clothes. I just slip off my sneakers and socks and crawl under the sheets. I pull the blanket over my head like a tent. I know it isn't any real protection, but it makes me feel safe. It is like when I was a little kid and used to make pretend longhouses under card tables draped with curtains. No one could see me.

"Help me," I whisper as I settle down to sleep. And this time it's not just a generalized plea to the universe. I'm speaking to my dreams.

11

RUNNING

A S I HIDE UNDER the covers, I feel as if I am never going to go to sleep. The thought that eyes might be watching me, that a camera might be looking down from overhead makes me as tense as a guitar string about to be plucked. I close my eyes tight against that thought and I clench my fists. I'm not just scared; I'm also angry and frustrated. How am I ever going to fall asleep?

Suddenly the covers are whisked away from me. I jump up with a yell. I'm ready to resist however I can. I'll kick and bite and scratch. Even though my so-called uncle is bigger than I am, I won't give up without a fight. I blink my eyes, trying to bring the shadowy world into focus, step back with my hands still held up . . . and bump into something big and hard and rough. I spin around and find myself face-to-face with the trunk of a giant tree.

A tree? How did a tree get into the room? And, for that matter, where has the room gone?

"Little Sister," says a voice from behind me. It is not a human voice. Yet it is a voice I welcome. I know who it is even before I turn around.

As I do, I realize that I'm back in deerskin clothing with moccasins made of thick moose hide.

"Little Sister!" the rabbit says again. This time it sounds as impatient as a parent trying to get the wandering attention of a child.

"Yes," I say.

"You must keep running," the rabbit says. It points with its left paw toward a direction that I somehow know to be the direction of the sunrise.

"The one who seeks to devour you is close on our trail. Follow me."

The rabbit begins to run and I follow close behind. I've only taken a few steps when a scream splits the night. It is so terrible—and so close—that I stumble. But I don't fall. I just run harder. The rabbit is leading me though the dark forest. There is just enough light from the moon, her face like that of a grandmother trying to help her little ones see their way.

She isn't just lighting *our* way, though. I can hear heavy feet thudding behind us. We run and run. We run through a glade of great pine and cedar trees and down a hill into a ravine thick with brush. We force our way through tangles of saplings and blackberry bushes. We leap over fallen logs, splash through a swamp thick with ferns, climb one hill and then another. How long we run, I don't know. I seem to be able to run without getting winded as I would in the waking world. But we are not getting away. The heavy feet keep thudding behind us.

Then I begin to hear something else. It is water. The rabbit leads me headlong down a trail that looks familiar to me. I've been in this place before, not in my dreams but in the waking world. I can tell by the giant stones and the lake that glitters in the valley off to our right and the shape of the land. It's the park where my father and mother used to take me sometimes on picnics. It's only about two miles from the house of my so-called uncle. But things are different. In the waking world there are roads and sidewalks and benches. Here there are only old tall trees and a deer trail. Still, I know where we're going. Toward the river just above the big waterfall.

Moonlight gleams on the river just ahead of us as we begin to scramble down a steep slope. The river is high, higher than I've ever seen it before. But the swinging suspension bridge that I've always loved, the bridge I've crossed so many times, is not there. Of course it's not there, a voice inside me says. This is long ago, even if it isn't far away.

But if there is no bridge, how are we going to get across the river?

We're right on the bank now, and the rabbit stops. It stands up to its full height, looking one way and then the other, as if confused. Did it expect a bridge here, too? What kind of spirit guide is the rabbit, anyhow?

"What can we—" I start to say. But I don't finish my question. The howl that rips apart the night air is so loud, so full of hunger, that it makes me spin around and fall to one knee.

The creature is there, on top of the slope above us. He's no more than a hundred yards away from us, and the light of the moon that shone so gently on me is stark and hard in the way it lights up the creature that looms there above me. He is taller than a tall man. He wears tattered buckskin clothing, clothing that hangs from him in shreds. But he has no need of clothing to warm his flesh, for whatever flesh he once had is gone. Shiny white bones can be seen through the rips in his buckskin shirt, and his head is a glistening skull.

But even though he is a skeleton, he has eyes. His eyes are green and burn like strange flames, and there is a darkness about his teeth that I'm sure is dried blood. The creature turns his head, as if sniffing the air. Then he stares down toward us and he opens his mouth in a wide grin. He raises his arm and points down toward us. Correction, toward me. For when I look around for my guide, I realize that the rabbit has disappeared,

"My niece," the Skeleton Man cries, in a voice that is both scream and whisper, "I am coming for youuuuu!"

I'm ready, more than ready, to wake up now.

12

ACROSS THE LOG

S THE SKELETON MAN starts down the hill toward me, he seems to have a hard time keeping his balance on the steep slope. Waving his long arms, he begins to slide. His bony feet are too slippery! He begins to fall and then, crashing through the brush and fallen limbs, he rolls right past me and splashes into the river.

"We have to keep running," says a voice next to me. I look down. It's the rabbit.

"Where were you?" I ask. I'm really upset that it deserted me.

"I knew the creature would fall," the rabbit says. "That is why I took us down this trail. But he has not been killed. He will climb out of the river again and follow us. Hurry, I have found the place where we can get across."

The rabbit starts up a trail I hadn't noticed before. We climb higher and higher. A roaring sound is getting louder and louder. Then I realize what I am hearing, and I know where we are. We're going up toward the top of the falls where the river is nar-rower. There is another bridge there in my time, one that a road goes over. But what will be there now?

I am panting hard when we reach the top of the steep trail.

"Oh no," I say as I see what we have to cross.

"Oh yes," says the rabbit.

I look hard at the rabbit, for it sounds as if it's mak-ing fun of me. But all it does is keep pointing with its paw toward the place where we must go. There is nothing more than a dead tree that has fallen across the river, right over the falls. Even though the tree was tall enough to reach the other side, its trunk isn't that thick. Going across will be like walking on a tightrope.

The moonlight glistens on the white foam of the water striking the rocks far below. It is a long way down. I've heard that when you fall in a dream you always wake up before you hit the bottom. I don't want to find out if this is true. I also have a feeling that this dream isn't just any dream. If I get hurt in this dream, I think it won't just be a scary memory when I wake up—if I wake up.

I want to protest again, but there's no time. The rabbit is already halfway across and I know that I have to follow. I've never been afraid of heights. After all, I'm the daughter of a Mohawk man who worked the high iron before he went into the banking business and met my mom. My dad and other Mohawks like him built places like the World Trade towers. But even though I'm not usually afraid of heights, I've never done anything like this before. Maybe, I think, I could crawl across. I stand there, not ready to put even one foot on that tree trunk.

"Ayyyyy-aaaahhhh!"

The scream is now so close that I am on the log before I have time to decide whether to go over it upright or on my stomach with my legs wrapped around it. I don't walk across, I run! Maybe it is foolish to turn around to look, but when I do I see I was almost too slow. Skeleton Man is there, standing on the other bank, one bony foot already on the log. He holds out his arm and points at me.

"My niece," he whispers, "I am coming for you."

The rabbit nudges my leg with its paw.

"Don't run now," the rabbit says. "Wait."

Skeleton Man is coming across the log now, taking one step at a time, his eyes boring into mine. I feel as if I'm being hypnotized, but I can't let that happen. I know what I have to do. Another step and I still wait, another step, another, and now he is in the middle. I tear my eyes away from him, go down onto one knee, and push the end of the log as hard as I can.

"Noooo!" Skeleton Man howls.

But he is too late. The end of the log slips off the bank into the water, twists as the current catches it, and then goes tumbling over the falls, carrying Skeleton Man with it toward the sharp rocks below.

I open my eyes before he hits the bottom. It was all a dream, the whole thing. I'm safe in my bed and it's morning, and I feel great. I can see a crack of light coming in through the closed curtains. I jump out of bed and throw open the curtain, certain that I'll see my mom's autumn flower bed with its birdbaths and feeders, my old swing set, and the little willow tree Dad and I planted.

But the morning sunlight doesn't show me that at all. My heart sinks again as I see below me a dreary backyard where nothing wants to grow and the tall, bent-shouldered shape of my uncle walking toward his toolshed. I step back from the window before he can catch a glimpse of me, and I sit down on the floor. Nothing has changed.

I get up and go into the small bathroom. I try

not to even think about the possibility of another camera being in there, but just in case, I keep a big towel wrapped around me as I wash up and get dressed.

13

TOMORROW

As I walk into Ms. Shabbas's classroom, she gives me a very big smile and mouths the words, "We'll talk later."

I nod to her and smile. The door to my room was unlocked this morning after all, just like every other morning. Breakfast was waiting for me on the table. A blue bowl with cornflakes in it, a glass of milk, and a smaller glass of orange juice—all so neatly laid out that it looked like something in one of those old situation comedies about happy families that they rerun on cable. Except no mother and father. My so-called uncle was nowhere to be seen. I sat down just like a normal kid. Then I looked around furtively in every direction and shoved all of the food into my backpack.

And now I'm safe in school. Everything is like it always is here. The only thing different is the workmen. They're sloppy, leaving their tools all over the place. And here I am in my own classroom, a place so safe-feeling that it is unreal to me. I look around, blinking my eyes to make sure I'm not imagining it.

Will Ms. Shabbas believe me when I tell her about my seeing those television monitors? Or about the camera I think may be hidden in my light fixture? Will that make me sound ultra-paranoid or what? I know she's on my side and I want to tell her. But then I also know what the rabbit told me in my dream about my parents being buried and that I have to save them. If I tell Ms. Shabbas about the cameras, she'll take me away and then I won't be able to save them. Somehow I feel that I have to do it by myself.

Today Ms. Shabbas doesn't forget to sing. It's that song about Annie that I sang myself to sleep with. "Tomorrow." She looks right at me as she sings about how it is going to be better on the day after this one. I know she is telling me that she is still on my side, that I have to buck up, keep a stiff upper lip, not give up the ship. She loves songs and stories that have upbeat endings. Mention the *Titanic* to most people and they think of a tragic love story. Mention it to Ms. Shabbas and she will start belting out something from *The Unsinkable Molly Brown*. Molly, just like me. Except I am not named for some survivor of a shipwreck. I'm named Molly after Molly Brant, a Mohawk warrior woman from the eighteenth century. "Back during the American Revolution," my mom told me, "one word from Molly Brant went farther than a thousand words from any white man. No one ever got the best of Molly Brant."

For some weird reason, Ms. Shabbas and her up-with-people singing helps me. Corny-but-sincere is her style, and it is just what I need this morning. I want to get out of my seat and walk up and hug her while she is singing. Instead I just give her a thumbs-up sign when she is done. She winks at me.

But when the time comes for us to talk, I still don't tell her anything. I need her to be on my side, and I'm too scared she won't believe me. Nothing new, I say. Which is true. It's just that now I know my so-called uncle has been keeping watch on me through a camera lens.

"Will you be okay over the weekend, honey?"

The weekend starts tonight. Every kid in America but me is looking forward to the weekend. I have a feeling that whatever awful thing he has in store for me is going to happen tomorrow. I swallow hard and make myself smile.

"I'll be fine," I say.

"Should I come over and check in on you?"

"If you have time."

"I'll make time on Sunday."

And that is how we leave it. She will call my so-called uncle after school and let him know she is going to come over to visit on Sunday. She's going to take me out for lunch and a visit to the park. If nothing else, it will let him know that someone is watching and that he won't get away with it.

But the small measure of relief I feel is short-lived. Maybe, I think, he doesn't care if he gets away with it. If he is crazy or evil, maybe getting caught wouldn't bother him. If he gets caught after doing whatever he plans to do to me, that won't help me much, will it?

Sunday. That leaves all of tonight and all of to-morrow and tomorrow night. Sunday may be too late for me.

TOOLSHED

W HEN THE SCHOOL DAY ends, I hang back from the crowd of kids who head out the door. They're happy about the weekend. For them the clock's hands have been almost standing still, while for me they've been going double time. Like my brain is going around and around like a top that's out of control. But it has kept circling back to one idea. It is a crazy one, but the only one I've been able to come up with.

Like the kids, the workmen have been eager for the day to end, too. They've even left before us. That's my first real break, that and the fact that they've left their toolboxes open again. Sure, they put a yellow ribbon across the hall in front of the library to keep people out. You know how easy it is to duck under a yellow ribbon? And though my backpack is a lot heavier when I get on the bus, no one notices.

When I get off the bus, I stand for a long time looking down the darkening road. I feel so scared. I should run away now. But where? And what good would it do me? Not only that, but for some reason I feel as if running away now won't just affect me, but my whole family. My real family.

Dinner is waiting on the table for me. It's pizza, and it looks good and smells even better. And there's an open bottle of Coca-Cola, too. My favorite drink. I sit down and look at the pizza and then I shake my head. I won't eat any of this dinner, either.

"What's wrong?" My so-called uncle's whispery voice comes suddenly from behind me and it makes me jump. I turn and see him in the doorway, standing with his back to me. "Feeling sick again?" he says. There is a tone to his voice that worries me. It isn't concern; it's sarcasm. It is like he is saying that he knows more than I do, that he knows what is going to happen and I don't. I hope he is wrong.

"I'm just tired," I answer.

I take my bag and go upstairs and go into my room and lock the door. I take a book out of my bag and try to read it. The letters of the words all look like strange insects crawling over the page. But time doesn't crawl by. Before long it is dark outside. I turn out the light in the room and wait.

His footsteps come up the stairs and pause for a long time, too long, in front of the door. When the *snick* of the outside lock comes, I start breathing again. I stuff the pillows under the covers to make it look like I'm in there. I crouch in the shadowiest corner by the window. I start counting the times I breathe in and out. I am up to three thousand four when I hear the sound of the door downstairs. Yes, I think. It's just as I hoped. He's keeping to the same routine he follows every night. He always spends time in that toolshed before he comes up and goes to bed. I peek out the lower corner window and see his shadowy shape cross the yard and the light go on in his toolshed.

My feet don't want to move. "Now," I say to them. With small, timid steps I make my way over to my backpack, open it, and fish around for what I want, a heavy thing with a pistol grip. I pull it out. A power screwdriver. The door may be locked, but the hinges are on the inside.

The whirring of the drill sounds terribly loud, even though I keep telling myself it isn't. I stop everything and listen. I don't hear anything and I continue. One screw, two, three. The screws are long and heavy, and I put each one into my pocket as it comes out. I have to get up on my toes to reach the top ones. I drop the fifth screw and it hits the floor with a loud *thwack*. Again I stop work and listen. But all I hear is silence. I start breathing once more.

Finally the last screw is removed. I stand up and take the foot-long crowbar from my pack. I pry it between the jamb and the door. The door pops free with a soft *thump*. I grab hold and pull it toward me, and the locks slip out. Now that it is free on both sides, the door almost falls over, but I lean my shoulder against it and manage to prop it against the doorjamb. I slip out and pull my pack out after me. I can't get the door exactly back into place where it was, but by leaning it a little I make it look like it is still closed.

I should have looked out the window before I left the room to see if light was showing under the toolshed door. But it is too late for that now. I put the pack over my shoulder and then start down the stairs, stepping sideways on each stair to try to keep them from creaking. It takes me a year to reach the bottom.

Now I'm only a few steps from the front door. But that is not where I am heading. I need evidence. I head for the room with the computer in it. There has to be something in there that I can take and use as proof, proof that my uncle isn't who he says he is, proof that I really am in danger.

The door is open again and that same light is shining from the computer screen. But I don't focus on that. Instead I turn to the pile of glossy pages next to the keyboard. I turn one over and it almost makes my heart stop beating. It is a photo of my mother. And it is not an old picture but a recent one. How do I know that? Because she is wearing the same brand-new blouse she was wearing the last day I saw her and Dad go out the door. But she doesn't look exactly the same as she did on that day. On that day she didn't have her hands tied together and she wasn't leaned back against the rough board wall of a shed and she didn't have a piece of duct tape over her mouth.

HARD EVIDENCE

I STOP LOOKING AT pictures after finding the one of my mother. Things are starting to make more sense and no sense at all. All I know is that I have to take the whole stack of pictures from his computer desk. I put them into the folder in my backpack. There's other stuff on his desk, too. Lists of things that have to do with databases and hacking into computers like the one at the bank where Dad works. I grab that stuff and then add a handful of computer disks lying on the desk. I zip the pocket tight and put the backpack over my shoulder. Once I get rid of the tools it won't be that heavy to carry. But I don't take out the rest of the tools I've borrowed from school. Not yet. I kneel down and make sure that my sneakers are tied and double knotted. I'm not going to change my plan about getting to the outside phone booth near the park entrance where I can call Ms. Shabbas, but I am going to add one thing to it.

I walk out the back door toward the toolshed. I've looked at that yard so many times from my window, but I've never been in it before. It is his place and he told me to stay away from it. Not that he needed to. Until now I've tried to avoid anyplace where he might be.

There are decorative stones on the ground that used to be part of the abandoned overgrown garden. They are white and round and the size of golf balls. I pick up three of them. I'm a good runner, maybe the best in the school, but I'm no pitcher. I might miss on the first throw.

But I don't. The stone sails through my upstairs

window with a crash that is as satisfying to me as it is loud. I don't need to throw another stone. He's heard it, and he comes out of the toolshed moving so fast that it scares me. He doesn't move like an old man but like some kind of big cat. He looks in all directions and seems to be sniffing the air. But he doesn't see me or smell me hiding behind the cedar bush next to the shed. He stares at the house and then lopes across the yard and goes inside.

I'm counting under my breath as I dart into the toolshed. When I get to a hundred, I tell myself, I'll turn and run no matter what. It is so clean and neat inside, the shelves are spotless, the tools hung on Peg-Boards. It's mechanical. It doesn't look as if a human being has ever been in here. Ten, eleven, twelve. I see that the back wall is at a funny angle. I try to push it and it moves like a door and then sticks. Thirteen, fourteen, fifteen. I pull out the crowbar and pry it open. There's a small room behind it with a dirt floor. But its not just dirt. In the middle of the floor is something that looks like a ring. Twenty-two, twenty-three. I kneel by the ring, brush dirt away, and see that it is connected to a trapdoor that is held shut by a hinged metal strap that fits over a thick metal staple. I pull out the pin that holds it shut. Then I take a deep breath and pull on the ring. The door is heavy, but it slowly begins to move. Dirt hisses off as I lift it. There's another door, a metal grating fastened with a padlock. But I can look down through it into the dark room hollowed out like a cave under the toolshed.

"Hello," I hiss. Twenty-seven, twenty-eight.

A hand reaches up to touch the grating. I recognize that hand.

"Dad," I whisper. Our fingers touch, link briefly before he falls back. My heart is pounding. It's really him! He's alive. There's so much I want to say, but I can't make my voice come out. And in the back of my mind I remember that I must keep counting. Thirty-one, thirty-two, thirty-three. I swallow the lump in my throat and manage to ask the question that I have to ask, even if I'm afraid of what the answer might be.

"Where's Mom?"

"She's here," he answers. His fingers push mine away. "Run."

"Is she all right? Are you all right?"

"Run, Molly," he says again. "There's no time. Get away!"

"No, Dad, not yet," I whisper. And as I say it I feel a certainty and strength like I've never felt before. I know what I have to do and I am going to do it.

I've got the bolt cutter out now. I maneuver it around to the lock that holds the grating and press down with all my strength. The jaws of the bolt cutter shear through the steel, as if it was butter. Fifty-seven, fifty-eight, fifty-nine.

"Run," Dad says again. "Now!"

"The falls, Dad," I whisper. "You know the place."

I push the bolt cutter and every other tool I have in my bag through the grating. I've lost count now. I don't know if there's enough time. I'm sure that by now he will have gone upstairs to my room. But the way he moved like a cat, so fast, makes me uncertain now how long he'll take.

I'm through the hidden door, the door of the toolshed is ahead of me. But I don't go through it straight. I duck and twist as I come out, and it's a good thing because he is there waiting in the darkness and he almost grabs me. His bony fingers slip through the loose braid in my hair. I scream and yank and I'm free. I go around the house toward the road. Just as I expected, he has gone around the other side to cut me off. He thinks I'm going to run toward town, toward other houses because his is the last house on the road. He's wrong. I'm going the other way, running fast. Running and running.

I venture a quick look back to see where he is. He isn't far behind me, no more than fifty yards. The moonlight glitters off his white forehead. Suddenly a rabbit darts out of the bushes and crosses in front of him, making him stumble. I gain another twenty yards, running and running. Looking back will only slow me down. I won't risk that again. I feel the strength of that story from long ago in my legs. I won't get tired.

I run and run and keep running. I have gone at least a mile now. The lake glitters in the moonlight off to my right and the Visitors' Center is just ahead of me, but there's no time now to use the phone. I pass the sign for the park, turn onto the trail, and begin to climb. I can no longer hear him behind me. This is my territory now. I'm sure I know it better than the one chasing me.

But I don't. I round the corner where the trail is narrow and the cliff falls off to the right. He is there ahead of me, cutting me off. There is a grin on his skeletal face, and his long arms are spread wide as if in welcome.

16

ESCAPE

Y OU CAN'T ESCAPE ME," he says in a hollow voice, a taunting voice. "Can you, little niece?"

If I try to answer him, I'll be done for. It would be like a mouse trying to argue with an owl. Instead I throw my backpack at him and, as he staggers back a step, I scramble up the slope off the trail into the brush. The trail edge is thick with blackberry bushes. They scratch at my hands and my face. Dead thorns stick through my jeans into my knees. But I get low, as low as a rabbit, and I crawl through and under the brush.

He can't. I hear him being held back by the thorny branches. I crawl until I find a clear area, then I stand up and move as quickly as I can along the dark, wooded slope. I roll my feet as I step like Dad taught me so that I don't make much sound. Then I stop and listen. I don't hear anything for a few heartbeats and then . . .

"Whooooo!" It's like the cry of an owl just below me on the trail. But it's not an owl, even though it makes me want to jump like a little mouse being scared out of hiding. "Whoooo!" Skeleton Man calls again. "I'm waiting for youuu. I will get youuuuuuu."

I don't move. I'll sit here all night if I have to. I won't let him scare me into showing myself. Silence. Nothing but silence for a long time. Too much silence, for it means that other things in the woods that would normally be making noise at this time know something is still out there. Something dangerous. Like me, they're waiting.

Then I see it. A beam of light coming through the forest. It is sweeping back and forth, not at random but moving slowly, patiently. He has a flashlight. Its illumination is moving toward me, its beam like the strand of a spider's web that will catch me. It's getting too close, and I have to move. I crawl downslope as slowly as I can, a hand's width at a time, until I reach the trail. Then I'm up and running toward the falls again. I'm not making much noise, but I begin to hear the feet of Skeleton Man thumping on the hard-packed earth of the trail behind me.

"Whoooo," he cries. "Whooooooo. I'm coming for youuuuuu!"

There's a place just ahead of us, around the next corner, where I remember my father and I had to duck under the long, low limb of a maple tree that overhung the trail. I'm praying that no one has trimmed that branch as the path bends around the hill. Yes! The branch is leaning over the narrow trail just as I'd remembered. I grab it as I run and it bends with me. Still holding it, I turn slightly. He's too close! He's about to grab me, but when I fall back and let the branch go, his hand misses me. The branch whips back to strike him in the face, knocking him off balance onto one knee and onto the loose stones at the steep edge of the trail. He begins to slip, and for a moment, it seems as if he is going to slide all the way off the trail into the deep ravine below. But, at the last moment, he whips one bony arm out, grabs the branch, and starts to pull himself back up. Before he can get to his feet I'm up and running again.

As I run I startle something that had been hiding in the brush next to the path. It runs ahead of me, clearly visible in a band of moonlight shining through the overhanging branches. It's a rabbit again. I know there are rabbits all through the park. You hardly ever walk through here in the morning or early evening without seeing at least four or five of them. It's not at all likely that it is the same one that slowed down my pursuer back near the house. But something in me tells me different, tells me that it's the same rabbit and it is trying to help me. It runs ahead of me and then suddenly darts off the main path onto a smaller, even steeper trail.

I know where this trail leads. It might seem like a dead end to some people if they just read the signs that say TRAIL CLOSED and BRIDGE OUT on them. But I can see that the wooden-planked suspension bridge over the gorge is still there. Its boards are old, but it should be able to hold my weight. I follow the rabbit up that trail, my feet slipping on the loose stones, my hands grasping at branches and clumps of grass as I climb.

Just as I'd remembered, there is a hole in the bottom of the chain-link fence big enough to crawl through. It was probably made by the local kids who carried up the narrow pieces of plywood to lay over the spots in the long, swaying bridge where the boards have rotted and fallen away, down into the stream, which is nothing more than a thin band of silver among the jagged rocks far below. But it doesn't look as if even the daredevil kids from the high school have ventured across the bridge for a long time.

I drop to my knees and crawl under the fence. A sharp piece of wire scratches my cheek and I feel the blood flow down my face. Another wire catches on my pant leg and I pull as hard as I can. I can't be caught here.

"WHOOO!" The eerie scream comes from right behind me and then there is a crash as his headlong rush takes him right into the chain-link wire. I feel something grabbing at my foot. I pull free, leaving my sneaker behind.

There's no time to stop or think. I start across the bridge, my arms spread out to hold the rusty cables on each side, my eyes looking down to see where to place my feet. One step, two, three. Old boards creak under my feet and the bridge begins gently swaying back and forth. Four, five, six. The rhythm is almost like that of a dance. Nine, ten, eleven, twelve, and I'm almost halfway across.

"Molly." The harsh whisper that cuts through the night from behind me makes me take a wrong step. My foot goes right through a rotten board. He's never spoken my name before, and the chill that it sends down my spine makes me shake all over. "Come back here."

I can't stop myself. I turn around and look. He's standing there, back at the end of the bridge, perhaps hesitant to cross it. His long arms are held up above his head, his fingers spread out so wide that they look like the talons of a giant bird. The moonlight glistens off his pale hard face and the top of his head, and it seems as if there is no skin at all. His eyes are twin blue flames burning from within his skull.

"No," I say, not just to him, but to myself. I wrench my foot free, break away from his hypnotic gaze, and start forward again. There's a thin piece of plywood just ahead spanning the last ten feet.

Suddenly the bridge starts to shake. I know that he is on it, moving across to catch me. And he's coming fast. I'm on the plywood now and it bends, almost to the point where the end that overlaps the concrete lip at the end of the bridge slips free. But it doesn't. I reach the safety of the other side. Then I keep myself from doing the one thing I want to do—which is to scream for help and run headlong, run as fast as I can to get away from the bony hands that I know are about to reach out and grab me. Instead, I turn and drop down onto the ground and kick my heels against the edge of the piece of plywood. And even though he's already on it, the plywood slips—*fwap!*—past the lip of stone.

The plywood falls from beneath him, sails down into the gorge like a flipped playing card. He pitches forward, his long fingers clawing forward wildly. I try to pull myself back, but one clawing hand wraps around my ankle. It holds on so hard that I feel a searing pain, as if I'm being burned by those fingers. I begin to slide back toward the edge. I'm about to be pulled into the gorge with him! I grab hold of a metal bar that sticks up from the concrete. My arms feel as though they're being torn from my shoulders, but I don't let go. Instead I kick at the fingers with my other foot, the foot that still has a sneaker on it. Those fingers are strong, but they are bone, nothing but bone, and I'm alive, and I am stronger than Skeleton Man. I won't let him defeat me now. I kick again and again and then . . .

The clawed fingers wrapped about my ankle slip free. I hear the one last despairing cry of "Noooooooooo" as Skeleton Man falls away from me like a bad dream disappearing when you wake.

My own hands are slipping. But after all I have been through, I can't fail now. I won't let myself fall. I dig in my fingers. My sneakered foot finds a rock for leverage as I push and claw my way up to the top, away from the brink. My heart is pounding like a drum, but I am alive. I breathe in and out as I look at a sky that is filled with the light of the moon and stars. After a while, I inch my way back to the edge and look over. All I can see is darkness and the thin, glittering line of the stream far below, a ribbon of silver touched by the light of the moon. I rub the place where Skeleton Man's fingers scratched my ankle. I can hardly believe it, but I'm perfectly safe at last.

"Molly," a deep voice calls from the main trail below me. "Molly." That voice is worried, almost frantic, but it makes my heart leap with joy.

"I'm here, Dad," I answer. "I'm coming."

Then I go leaping down the trail, my feet as sure as those of a mountain goat. I feel like I can't fall, but even so I stumble just before I reach him.

But he doesn't let me fall. Powerful arms catch me and lift me up, right off the ground, and then my dad is hugging me.

"You saved us, Molly," he whispers into my ear.

"You're our Warrior Girl."

"Dad," I sob back. I don't feel like a Warrior Girl at all, just a little kid who wants to cry and cry and cry.

I wish I could say they found my so-called uncle. But they didn't, not on the rocks below or in the swift-running stream. Even though the water was high and the current would have carried him down into the deep lake, they should have found him. But they didn't. Where his body went remains a mystery.

So does his real identity. I found my backpack on the trail where I threw it at him, but none of the evidence I gave them and nothing he left in the house gave any clue. They found the doctored photographs, the phony identification papers, all of the stuff in the computer, including the way he was able to hack into banks and databases to get money and information about people. It appeared that he'd chosen our family because of Dad's job with the bank and because he could use me and Mom as leverage to make Dad give him the information he needed.

The fact that we didn't have any relatives made it easier for him to deceive people about being my uncle. There was also a diary, with photographs, of how he'd planned everything and carried it out. It was all there, from posing as a highway patrolman to stop their car while they were on their way home that Saturday night to stepping in as my next of kin. Everything was there except who he was and why he did it. And what he was planning to do with us in the end.

"What was it," the school psychiatrist said to me, "that made him want to have total control over a family like that? Was it a chemical imbalance? Perhaps it was because of things that happened to him as a child. Or perhaps not." Then she tapped her pencil against her chin and looked wise. Right.

I remember what my dad and mom said to me about it all when the police and the reporters and the lights and cameras were finally gone, and there was time at last for us to be alone together.

"There's going to be a lot of people talking about this, trying to figure it all out," Dad said. "But it seems to me that the only place where it makes sense is in our old stories." As he spoke I realized how much the voice of the rabbit in my dreams had been like his voice. "There are still creatures that may look like people but are something else. The reason creatures like Skeleton Man do what they do is that they like to hunt us. The only way to defeat them is to be brave."

He smiled at me then, and I smiled back.

I looked over at my mother and she nodded. But I could tell she had something more to say about it, too, about why he locked them up under the tool-shed and barely fed them, why he pretended to be my uncle. Dad and I didn't ask her; we just waited for her to speak.

"Molly," she said, holding my hand tight, "you know what a cat does when it catches a mouse? It doesn't kill it and eat it right away. It plays with it for a while first."

And that was all she had to say about it, though Dad reached over and took both of our hands and we sat there together like that for a long time.

Maybe, like Ms. Shabbas said to me, there never was any real why about it. "Honey," she said, "it happened, but now it is *over*." Then she sang a few lines from that musical about Don Quixote. "Yes, indeed," she said, nodding. "You have dreamed the impossible dream."

I can live with that. Like one of the old stories I've grown up with, something evil came into the lives of good people and we found a way to defeat it. My dad and mom and I are together again, we are happy, and that is enough for me.

THE RETURN OF SKELETON MAN

PROLOGUE

I HATE SEQUELS. I know that some kids love them, but not me. Once a story is over I'd just like it to be done with. Finis, as my teacher, Ms. Shabbas, puts it. But every time you go to a movie these days it seems like half the stuff showing is either sequels or sequels of sequels or even, like in those newer *Star Wars* films, prequels. All that ever gets better are the special effects. I ask you, though: After you've seen one planet blown up, what can you do to top that?

I want to say "Give me a break!" to those producers and directors. "Do something new."

The horror movies, of course, are the worst. *Halloween Part 2006. Friday the 13th Times Infinity.* It seems as if no matter what those sappy kids do to get rid of one of those mad-dog monsters like Freddy or Jason, he just comes back. You can shoot him, stab him, cut his head off, bury him, burn him, run him through a blender, make him into muffins, and nuke him in your microwave. It doesn't matter. There he is again, all knifey and bloodthirsty and ready to throw more buckets of gore in the petrified protagonist's face. You can even send Jason off to Hades and he'll still reappear—to fight Freddy in outer space or something equally weird. Once again, give me a break.

You might think I'm saying that sequels are boring and unrealistic. Well, they are. That was pretty much the way I used to think about them. But I have to confess, it is more than that for me now. What bothers me most about sequels now is not the thought that they're unrealistic. It's the fear that maybe they're true. Maybe some monsters really are

that hard to kill. Maybe, like poor old Jamie Lee
Curtis, I'll be going on with my life all la-la-la-la-la,
everything is fiiine. Until I turn a corner and find
him waiting for me.

1

ARRIVING

LOOK UP THERE, MOLLY. That's Sky Top Tower." I shift my gaze up, way up. There, far in the distance, at the top of a huge cliff, is a tall stone tower. I can hardly believe it. Here we are, on a late-autumn day, speeding along the New York State Thruway in the midst of a twenty-first-century seventy-mile-per-hour stream of traffic, dodging Winnebagos (the trucks, not the Indians) and people more interested in their cell phone conversations than in staying in their own lane, and I'm staring at something that looks like it belongs in a Dracula movie.

"Wow," I gasp. Then, just to show my parents how articulate I am, I say it again. "Wow!"

But I'm not the only one awed by the sight.

"Is that really where we're going?" my mom asks in a tone that indicates she hopes the answer is yes.

In the rearview mirror I can see the big grin that spreads over my father's face. He'd always loved to surprise us in the past, but over the last year or so, he's been avoiding springing things on Mom and me unexpectedly, which is understandable, considering the recent events we barely survived. I haven't seen that wide a smile on his face for months. It makes me so happy that I wiggle in my seat like a puppy.

"Uh-huh," Dad says in that slow, confident voice of his. "That's where the conference is taking place." He carefully checks his mirrors and puts on his blinker to move into the exit lane for New Paltz. "Well, not exactly in that tower. There's a huge old Victorian hotel on that mountaintop, just below the tower, with 251 rooms."

"Cool," I say.

Dad nods. "Way cool, indeed, Molly girl. It's called the Mohonk Mountain House, and when you are up there you feel like there's no place else in the world. Totally isolated in the middle of a vast forest preserve."

"Mohonk?" my mother asks. "Isn't that where they had the Friends of the Indian conferences back in the 1880s, honey?"

I lean back to listen. It's going to be one of those discussions between my mom and dad that's as much a seminar as a conversation. Some people might find it boring, but my dad is a natural storyteller and my mom has this way of explaining historical events that just makes them come alive for me.

I hug myself as I listen and look out the window. My dad explains that two brothers, the Smileys, started building the Mohonk Mountain House back in 1869. It began as one building, but wings got added on and it just kept getting bigger and bigger. All kinds of major events have taken place at Mohonk, starting at the end of the nineteenth century with the Friends of the Indian—who did do a lot to make things better for native people—right up to the present day. In recent years the Smiley family has added many modern facilities, from videoconferencing rooms to an Olympic-size ice-skating rink. The Mountain House restaurants are famous, and people come to the hotel from all over the world for weekend getaways. It's also a favorite place for business conferences like the seminars my father's bank is sending him to. This is his second visit but the first time we are joining him.

Their discussion pauses only when we go through the tollbooth; then we are off the thruway. The tower is out of sight now. We're heading into the town of New Paltz, one of those places that used to be surrounded by farms but is gradually sprawling out with development. There are the usual fast-food places and chain stores, but when we drive into the town itself it gets better.

"Ambience," Mom says.

I know what she means. The buildings are old and the storefronts are all different here. They reflect the kind of stuff you see in places dominated by a big university like New Paltz—trendy little ethnic restaurants, colorful hand-painted signs, and small, unique stores.

"Walking and shopping later this weekend?" Mom says, turning back for a moment to look at me, her own smile almost as big as my dad's was.

"Def!" I say. I can already picture Mom and me strolling down the streets, the warm autumn sun shining as we window-shop or have tea at that little place there, or check out that bookstore on the corner here.

It all seems too good to be true.

We're through the town now, passing over a bridge across a little river and taking a winding road that leads up the mountain. The Smileys, whose descendants still run the place, loved nature. So they bought up thousands of acres of the Shawangunk Mountain range just to keep it wild. Then, in 1969, they turned sixty-four hundred acres of their land into the Mohonk Preserve—which surrounds the Mountain House—the biggest private nature preserve in all of New York State.

"Wow!" is going through my head again. The glaciers that sculpted the Shawangunk range made spectacular cliffs everywhere. The narrow road we're following is winding back and forth like a snake along the tops of those sheer drops. I catch a couple of glimpses of the town and the roads below, but most of the time all I can see is an endless expanse of evergreen forest. Hemlock and pine and cedar and spruce.

"Like going back into the past, isn't it?" my dad says to us. He doesn't take his eyes off the road. My dad is Mr. Safe Driver. Both hands on the wheel. "Except for this little highway, it's kind of what it was like a thousand years ago when it was just our people and the land here."

"Not our people," my mom says with a little smile. History being her thing, she can't resist the opportunity to correct him. "This area was Lenape land, not Mohawk."

"Well," Dad says, "I'll bet there were Mohawk tourists back then, too. Now, check this out. Got your passport ready, Molly?"

He nods his head toward the little building that appeared ahead of us as we rounded the turn. Of course they don't ask us for passports. That's just my dad being corny. Polite people ask where we're going and then wave us through the gate after Dad says he's going to the seminar.

"A gatehouse?" Mom says. "Where are we, Beverly Hills?"

"Better than that, small-town girl," Dad replies.

I giggle. It's fun to see Mom and Dad teasing each other like this.

"Just you wait," Dad adds. "You ain't seen nothing yet."

And, just as he promised, when we get around the next corner I see exactly what he means. Rising ahead of us are wide lawns, little open-air structures scattered all over the place, stone walls, and gardens that even now, in late autumn, look amazing. But what is really mind-boggling is the actual Mountain House. A gigantic wooden building, it seems to rise up from the cliffs themselves. It is seven stories tall and it looks like something out of a gothic story. Porches sweep along the sides as it spreads out, just going on forever. Not only that, it is right next to a beautiful lake and mirrored by sheer cliffs on the other side of it. I feel as if we have driven into a fairy tale.

Dad pulls up in front. He stops and is about to get out to give his keys to the parking attendant. But I don't give him a chance to do that. I throw my arms around his neck from the backseat and give him the biggest hug.

"This is going to be the best vacation ever," I cry.

THE PATH

ITHOUGHT THIS PATH through the woods would be a shortcut. Mistake number one, because I seem to have taken a wrong turn somewhere or else the path has grown twice as long after dark as it was when I first found it before dinner. I'm not sure how much farther I have to go, and I do not have a flashlight. Mistake number two. But the moon was really bright when I left the main lodge, and I was only going to walk a little ways in the moonlight before coming back. No way did I expect that the full moon was going to go behind the big bank of clouds that came rolling up over the white stones of the Shawangunk Mountains. No way was it going to get so dark that I could barely see my hand in front of my face. No way? Way.

That was my third mistake, thinking there was no way I could get in trouble here. There's nothing threatening, nothing dangerous, nothing after me—except in my memory. It's safe here at this old, well-cared-for resort on the mountaintop. Isn't it?

I'm trying to move quietly. My steps, though, are far from quiet. Snow hasn't come yet, even though a storm that might bring a dusting of snow to the high slopes has been forecast. The dry, fallen beech leaves rustle as I walk. Thick old trees loom overhead, making this more like a tunnel than a path. Cedar twigs and cones crunch underfoot. I don't like making this much noise in the woods.

Be quiet, my father always says. *Move slow. Calm yourself down.*

So that is what I try to do. I take slower, more careful steps. I roll my feet, heel to toe, the way my father taught me. It works. I no longer sound like a three-legged moose. But now I can hear the pounding of my heart. It is so loud that it sounds like a drum. I am not calming myself down.

A song my homeroom teacher made up pops into my head:

> There's nothing more fearful than fear itself,
> So hang your neuroses back up on the shelf.
> You'll just be more afraid the more that you
>   fear,
> So lift up your chin and smile, my dear.

Isn't that a hideous song? But I actually find myself starting to sing it as I walk along. The moon has come out again. I can see the path ahead of me. I'm not sure how far away the big old hotel is, where my parents are waiting, but it can't be that far. I'm feeling better. I sing a little louder. It's like whistling in the dark to keep away something evil. Unless something evil likes the sound of whistling. Mistake number four.

I quickly shut my mouth. I stop walking. I've just heard the sound of something behind me. Not feet rustling through the leaves. Not the crackling of branches breaking as a heavy body thrusts its way through them. No, a far scarier sound than that. It is the dry *tschick-a-tschick* of bone against bone, accompanied by the wind-whistling sound of breath.

I turn to see a grinning skull face looming over me, its teeth dripping fresh blood. Long, bony hands reach out to grab me. I can't get away. A heart-stopping scream tears the dark fabric of the night.

BAD MEMORIES

I STRUGGLE TO ESCAPE from the grip of Skele-ton Man's hand. But it won't let go.

"Molly," a familiar voice says. "It's all right."

That's when I realize that the hand holding my shoulder is not all cold and made of bone. Its grasp is gentle. I realize that heart-stopping scream was my own. I open my eyes and look up into my mother's concerned face.

I sit up and look around. It's not night at all. I'm

not in the woods but safe inside our suite of rooms. It's only our third day here, but already it feels like home. Late-autumn sunlight is coming in through the window behind my mother's head. It shines through her hair in a way that makes it look almost like an angel's halo or the aura you see glowing around saints in old paintings. I take a deep, trembling breath and let it out. I'm remembering now. I was feeling tired after our rock climb and hike up through the Lemon Squeeze to the tower on Sky Top, so I decided to take a nap before dinner.

Mom puts her arms around me. "It was just a dream, honey," she says.

I hug her back and sit up.

"I'm okay," I say. I even manage to smile. Molly the warrior is regaining control. She's confident, pushing the other Molly, the one who is a wounded wimp, way into the background, maybe even out of the picture entirely. Or at least that is how I make it look. I know how much it hurts Mom to see me upset.

But she isn't ready to let it go yet. She studies my face. If my dad were here and not still deep in that afternoon discussion called, I kid you not, "Enron and the Perils of Accrual Accounting," he would be holding our hands in his, making our own little circle of strength. It's kind of a Mohawk Indian thing, that circle-of-strength idea. He learned it from his own grandparents when he was growing up on the reservation at Akwesasne, on the border between the United States and Canada.

"A circle," my father always says, "is the oldest shape and the strongest." His voice is deep and calm. "That's why we dance in a circle, just as the Rabbit People taught us to dance. When we are together in a circle, we can all see each other's faces. A real circle, a circle of love and caring and respect, can keep a family together. It can help you survive almost any threat."

My dad has always tried to pass along to me as much of our Mohawk heritage as possible, including the old stories. I've talked with my parents about those stories a lot over the past year. I'm grateful my dad told them to me because I think the lessons I learned helped me survive what I went through. There are two lessons in particular that helped me.

The first is that there really are monsters. They may have different names these days and wear different masks than in ancient times, but they can still kill you. Knowing that monsters do exist can help you recognize danger before it's too late. You'll realize you have to get out of the way and not just stand there like a fawn frozen in the middle of a four-lane highway while a semitrailer bears down on you at eighty miles an hour with its headlights blazing.

The second lesson is that even a child may be able to overcome or outwit a monster if she just keeps her wits about her and doesn't panic. Be brave and the monster may fall. That was how it was with me.

What the old stories fail to mention is the panic that comes later. When it ended, I was a mess, despite having been a heroine in the papers and featured in a spot on CNN for two days in a row: GIRL SAVES PARENTS FROM KIDNAPPER WHO POSED AS UNCLE. (Then she falls apart.)

I suppose it wasn't that bad. I am, after all, known for melodrama. It wasn't like I couldn't function on a day-to-day basis or that I got hysterical every time I heard a loud noise. It was the bad dreams. In those dreams, Skeleton Man came back to get me and there was no one there to help me, not even the rabbit.

What rabbit? I know some of you are probably asking that right now, as well as a lot of other questions. What is this crazy kid babbling about? Here I am, assuming you all know my story while I rattle on without making much sense.

That's the problem with a sequel. You need to know the backstory. I won't tell it all. But I'll hit the high points like they do on some of those TV police shows.

Previously in Molly's life I was just a normal sixth grader—if normal includes being Mohawk Indian and having a father with a Harvard MBA who works for a big bank and tells his daughter bloodcurdling old Indian tales. I have to tell you about one of those stories right now, because it is a big part of what happened to me.

That story is the one about Skeleton Man. He was a greedy, lazy uncle who sat around the fire in his longhouse all day waiting for his family to bring him food. One day, when no one was around and all the food in the pot was gone, he thought he saw something to eat that had fallen into the coals. He reached for it and burned his finger so badly that he stuck it in his mouth to cool the singed flesh. "Oooh, I have found something tasty," he said, meaning his own cooked finger.

So he ate it. Then, seeing how easy it was, he stuck his other fingers in the coals, cooked the flesh on them, and ate them one by one. But he was still hungry. So he ended up cooking his whole self until all that was left of him was a skeleton. Gross, I know, but I used to adore that story and ask my father to tell it again and again.

Then Skeleton Man, who was still hungry, lured other members of his family into the dark longhouse so he could kill them and cook them and eat them. They just went in, one by one, not realizing their relative's hunger and greed had turned him into a monster. Finally, only one little girl was left. She refused to come into the longhouse because she knew something was wrong with the one who had been her uncle. So Skeleton Man came out and began to chase her.

Tschick-a-tschick-tschick-a-tschick, that was the noise his dry bones made, rubbing together, as he pursued her. He might have caught her, but she was helped by a rabbit she had rescued from the river earlier. It led her through the darkness. It helped her keep one step ahead of the cannibal skeleton.

Finally, the rabbit showed her how to trick Skeleton Man into following her out onto a log that had fallen across the swift river like a bridge. When he was in the middle, she pushed the end of the log into the water. Skeleton Man fell in and was washed away.

Then she went back to the longhouse where all her relatives, including her mother and father, had been eaten. All that was left of them were bones. But the rabbit told her what to do.

"Put their bones together," the rabbit said. "Go outside the longhouse and push over that big dead tree. Just before it hits the longhouse call out these words." Then he told her the magic words.

That girl did just as the rabbit said. Just before the tree hit the longhouse she shouted out what the rabbit had told her.

As soon as she did that, all of her relatives were restored with the flesh back on their bones. They jumped out the door, happy and alive.

I was once like the girl in that old story. And not just because I'm a Mohawk, as she was. My parents had vanished without a trace about a year ago. And there was a monster in my story, too. Some people say he was just a man, an evil old man who pretended to be my long-lost uncle after my parents had disappeared, even though he turned out to be the one who kidnapped them and held them prisoner. He meant to do something terrible to all three of us and I am sure he would have if I hadn't escaped. I was even helped by a rabbit, who appeared in my dreams to guide me.

My so-called uncle fooled everyone except me. Social Services even sent me to live with him in a spooky old house where he locked me in my room every night. Maybe you remember seeing it on the news, how I escaped from that house and found the place where he was holding my parents captive, how he chased me through the dark until he fell through the old bridge over the gorge. That's where the TV news stories mostly ended. Except for the ominous little mention at the end of each telecast that "the kidnapper's body has not yet been found." It never was.

My father talked about the circle more than usual in the months after it all happened. Not right away, of course. Right after I saved them, we were all so excited and happy and relieved that there was no time to be upset or think too much about it. It wasn't until after we were safe that all three of us started to feel depressed and sad and Dad started talking so much about the circle and I started having bad dreams.

Mrs. Rudder, my school counselor, met with us. Of course, she suggested antidepressants for me. My mother suggested something else to Mrs. Rudder, which made my father laugh. It ended up with the three of us going into family counseling. We could talk about our fears together and not feel foolish.

Together, my dad says, we can overcome anything. Even bad memories like those that were coming back to haunt me after it all supposedly ended when Skeleton Man fell into the gorge.

Gradually, the bad dreams became fewer and then it seemed as if they were gone. I no longer woke up in the middle of the night screaming. It had been months since that happened. But here, at this safe, secure place, where they even have a gatehouse halfway down the mountain where everyone in a car has to stop and be logged in before they can go any farther, the dreams have returned. This last dream has been the worst of all.

"It's over," Mom says. "It was just a dream. He's not coming back."

"I know," I reply, keeping my voice calm.

But I hear another familiar voice saying something else to me. I'm not hearing it with my ears but deep inside my mind.

It's not over, that voice says. *Some dreams are more than just dreams.*

And I nod my head, knowing it to be true.

Some dreams, that rabbit voice continues, *are like this one I just sent you. They are messages and warnings.*

And even though it sends a shiver down my spine, I understand what this message, this warning, means.

Skeleton Man will return.

MY SO-CALLED UNCLE

OLLY," MY MOM SAYS, "get dressed, honey. Your father will be here soon and he'll want to use the bathroom."

That's one disadvantage of the suite we're in. Three people and only one bathroom. Being a man, my dad doesn't have to spend much time in there at all. Since he doesn't even have to shave—a lack of male facial hair is just one more advantage of an aboriginal heritage, he jokes—he spends even less time in there than the average man. But there are things that Mom and I each need to do, involving mirrors and brushes and sprays and all that. I'm the kind of girl who wishes it all just came in a bottle you could simply point at yourself and *phhsssshh!* put it all on with one spray. Instant full facial. But lately I am feeling better about the results. So I am now ready to take the time, even though I let out a heavy sigh.

Mom's laying out clothes for my dad to wear to dinner. She likes doing these "girly, wifely things" when we're all together like this because she doesn't usually get to do them every day. She has a master's degree in social work and has done everything from being a drug counselor in a prison to working with unwed mothers. Currently she is the head counselor at a youth camp for juvenile offenders. She is a tough cookie. Of the three of us, Mom seems to have been the least fazed by what we all went through. Then again, she has been faithfully going to a self-defense class for women two nights a week. No way does she plan to ever get kidnapped again without putting up a fight.

I study myself in the mirror. I've got this little crease between my brows that shows up when I'm worried. It's like an anxiety barometer and it's there now. But at least the only face I see in the mirror is my own. In one of the dreams I've started having again, I look into the mirror and see not just my own face but the cold face of Skeleton Man staring over my shoulder.

The one question people kept asking was, why did that strange old man do it? There are theories. The most common one has to do with money. He kidnapped my parents because of my father's job with the bank. He was trying to get my father to tell him information that he could use to get a lot of money. It all had to do with wire transfers and offshore accounts in the Cayman Islands. My mom and I were being used as leverage to get my father to do what he wanted. But my father kept stalling him because he knew in his gut what I also believe to be true. As soon as he got what he wanted, my so-called uncle would have killed all three of us.

The investigators found all the stuff they needed to prove that money transfer theory. They found the computers, the phony identification papers, even uniforms he had used to pose as a policeman, a phone company employee, and a security guard.

And they also found evidence that tied him to the disappearance over several previous years of other bank executives in other cities, along with their familes. None of those people were ever seen again. Each of those disappearances had been connected with the loss of large sums of money from their bank. Millions. But the theory, until our family escaped, had always been that those bank people had stolen the money themselves. Before us, there had never been any loose ends. Not even a dead body. I don't like to think about what might have happened to the bodies of those poor innocent people.

Despite all they discovered, the investigators never found anything that told them my so-called uncle's true identity. I don't like to think about that, either. It's bad enough that my dreams and the rabbit had told me that he wasn't a person at all.

"He is Skeleton Man," the rabbit said. "He is a hungry monster just pretending to be human."

A monster. The other theory the state police investigators came up with was that whoever he was, he didn't really do it for the money. He did it for the thrill of controlling people's lives—until it was time for their deaths. He enjoyed playing with us the way a cat toys with a mouse. Monsters—whether they are serial killers or creatures in our old stories—don't see the rest of us as human. They just see us as playthings. Maybe they don't even think of themselves as evil. But I do. I know there's real evil in the world.

But I also know there is good.

"If it wasn't for good," my mother says, "we human beings would have been wiped out a long time ago. Either the monsters would have gotten us or we would have killed each other off with greed and jealousy and anger. So we have to believe in good. We have to look for the good in ourselves."

Sometimes, like that rabbit who turned up in my

dreams speaking in a voice like my dad's, there's good outside us, too. There's this old Indian idea about spirit guides. There are forces in the universe that can help us if we prove worthy. They may take the shape of an animal or a bird and appear to us to aid us. That was what the rabbit did for me, just like the rabbit in the old story who helped the girl escape from Skeleton Man.

The thought of that rabbit makes me smile—just as I'm putting on my lipstick. As a result I get some on my teeth. Before I wipe it off with a tissue, I notice how much that red lipstick on my teeth looks like blood. My smile disappears. There's a knot in my stomach again.

I finish wiping off the lipstick and turn toward the bathroom door, where my father has appeared, waiting "patiently" and looking at his wristwatch.

"Hey," he says to my mother, "it's a new record. Molly girl managed to finish before I reached retirement age."

It's one of his corny jokes, but it's so normal that it makes me feel good again and giggle. I pretend to be angry and I elbow him in the side.

"Watch it there, warrior girl," he says with a groan. "The ribs you broke last time still haven't healed."

I love my family. We're together and having fun. There is nothing wrong. Life is good. So why am I so worried? And why does my father also have that little furrow between his brow?

BY THE LAKE

AD HAS GOTTEN READY even faster than usual, which has left us time for a leisurely stroll along the lake before dinner. Both Mom and I are wearing comfortable shoes, and the paths are all well cared for and easy to walk along. It's so warm today that we don't need heavy coats. The few remaining late-autumn flowers, mums and pansies, are beautiful.

So why does everything around me seem as if it

is transparent? Why do I feel as if I am walking on thin ice that might break any minute? Why do I feel as if I am being watched?

Stop it, I tell myself. I'm being an idiot. Is dwelling on the past all I can do?

I need to look at the beauty around me and feel good about being here. I look at an old tree—and notice how one branch is shaped almost like a huge hand about to grab me. I look at the big stones along the trail—and see how one of them has a jagged edge that is almost like a row of hungry teeth.

Quit thinking about dumb things, I command myself. Unfortunately, when you focus on not thinking about something, that is all you can think about. For example, try not to think about a blue elephant.

"Molly, where are you going?"

I hear my dad's voice at the same moment I feel his hand on my elbow, pulling me back onto the path. I'm so distracted that I've almost walked off the trail right over one of the low cliffs and into the lake. It was just absentmindedness, but I find myself remembering another one of our old Mohawk stories. It's about a monster who lurks underwater and lures unsuspecting people to come closer and closer—like sleepwalkers—until it can grab them and pull them under.

That's a scary tale to most people, but I find it strangely reassuring. It gives me an idea. If I can concentrate on what it would be like if there were a Mohonk Lake monster, it may not leave enough room in my mind to worry about . . . something else.

The Monster of Mohonk, I think. A horrible, terrible old lake creature. I build a picture in my mind of something like a cross between Barney the dinosaur and the snaky Loch Ness monster. In my imagination, it is always hungry, but no one seems to know it is there, even though picnic baskets and pet poodles left by the lake have a habit of disappearing.

When their parents are not around, children come down to the lake, drawn by the monster's hypnotic mind-call. They climb onto his fuzzy purple back. You can almost hear a merry-go-round playing in the background. He carries them out into the center of the lake while he grins back at them with a big, happy, toothless Saturday-morning-kids'-show smile. However (cue the ominous theme music), when they are far enough out he opens his mouth even wider. Now the horrified tots can see that behind his big goofy grin, set farther back in his mouth, are row after row of huge razor-sharp teeth, bigger than those of the shark in *Jaws*.

Ka-chomp, ka-chomp, ka-chomp!

"You're smiling," my mother says, looking at me. "I knew you'd feel more relaxed once we got outside."

It's true—I'm beginning to feel like my old, imaginative self. The image of that deadly, hungry but goofy lake creature is doing it for me. It fits right in with what my father always said when he told me our old Mohawk stories about monsters: "Molly girl, those monsters were big and dangerous and hungry . . . and stupid. You can use a monster's own weakness against it."

I imagine a girl—a girl who looks like me but a lot younger—who has hidden inside the big old hotel while all the other kids have gone out to play. From behind the curtains of her window she has seen the lake monster scarf down lunch baskets and lure in foolish children. No one believes her when she tells them what she has seen. So she knows it is up to her. Her big brother has brought a bag of illegal fireworks with him on their vacation. She connects them all together with a long fuse, then she goes down to the deceptively peaceful lake with all those firecrackers in a picnic basket. She notices bubbles rising to the surface about fifty feet out and she nods to herself.

Quickly she lights the long fuse, puts down the basket, and calls out in a loud voice, "Oops, I have forgotten something and now I have to run back to my room. But all of this delicious food will be safe here beside the lake, where nothing big and purple and hungry and stupid can get it."

Then she turns and runs as fast as she can.

She has taken only a few steps before she hears the slosh of water and a loud gulp. She turns back to look and sees nothing but ripples and a few bubbles moving away from shore.

Wha-boomp! There is a big underwater explosion. A little geyser shoots up from the center of the lake, followed by pieces of purple monster flesh.

I keep refining that story in my mind as we reach the steps that lead up into the main building. Maybe after the monster is destroyed that little girl does something magical. Maybe she sings a song or throws some sweetgrass into the water, then all of the kids that were eaten by the monster come bobbing up to the surface, alive and well, although coated with monster slime—along with a hundred happy, yappy poodles. They swim back to the shore, where their bewildered, overjoyed parents—and dog owners—are waiting for them.

I turn at the top of the steps to look at the lake and the cliff that rises above it. Then I look back at the huge old building itself, at its dark old wood and stone. I could wander the long, echoey hallways of this place for days and never see it all. There aren't just big meeting rooms and places where concerts and shows take place; there are also creaky stairways, balconies, and closed doors that probably lead down into basement rooms where no one goes. Mohonk Mountain House is spooky. In fact, I'd be surprised if it wasn't haunted by at least a ghost or three. But the thought of ghosts doesn't scare me.

Like the imaginary lake monster whose story I've been creating, spectral beings are a better alternative than the reality of what my parents and I actually survived. That was a real horror story—too real.

Just like that, with one careless thought, my whole reassuring scary fantasy vanishes as quickly and completely as a soap bubble broken by the breeze. The knot in my stomach grabs hold once more. Everything around me that had just seemed old and safely quaint has suddenly become ominous. I really am as afraid as a little kid left alone in a haunted house. There are lots of other people around me, people here for my dad's conference, and others who've come to eat in the famous dining room or take part in the other programs that are always going on here—like the Adirondack musicians named Quickstep who'll be playing in the Lake Room tomorrow night.

But now I am feeling totally alone in this crowd. I don't want to look at any faces for fear that one of those strangers might look familiar, that I might see the cold, calculating eyes of Skeleton Man staring at me. In fact, I feel right now as if someone is watching me from behind, from just above me. But I don't allow myself to turn and look up toward the landing. I push through the crowd, trying not to sob, trying to catch my breath.

There is one part of the old Mohawk story of Skeleton Man that I usually leave out, even though it was always in the version my father told me. It's the part that is freaking me out right now. It's the part where, after the monster seems safely gone and everyone has been rescued, that rabbit comes back and whispers something in the little girl's ear. You may already have guessed what it is.

"The monster is not really dead. Skeleton Man will come back again."

By the time I catch up to my parents, who had gotten only a little ahead of me, I've regained my composure. I even manage to paint a smile on my face before I get to them, but I'm no longer feeling happy as we walk along the hall to the main dining room. And I can still feel eyes watching my back.

DARK CORRIDORS

ORMENGHAST. THAT IS THE title of a trilogy of old fantasy novels I heard about when they were made into a TV miniseries a few years ago. It's about this ancient castle that is so large it stretches for miles, with dark corridors and hidden rooms and strange characters. There's all kinds of murder and intrigue in the story.

This looks like Gormenghast was my first thought when we drove around the corner in our car and I saw where we were staying. Admittedly, it wasn't miles long, but it was huge and it looked even bigger, being way up on top of this mountain.

"Heeeere's Johnny," my father said, leering at my mother as we walked down the corridor toward the registration desk.

"Stop that," my mother said, trying not to laugh.

"All work and no play makes Jack a dull boy," my father replied in a mock creepy voice.

My mom punched him in the arm.

"Ouch," he said, pretending to be hurt.

"Next time it's the baseball bat," Mom answered.

I love it when my parents do that kind of thing. My dad likes to quote lines from scary movies and pretend to be the monster in them. Right then he was imitating Jack Nicholson in that movie *The Shining*, where this guy and his wife and little son go all alone to an old resort hotel way up in the mountains because he is the winter caretaker, but he gets driven crazy by the ghosts there and tries to kill his family.

For a while, after Skeleton Man, my parents stopped playing that game. I think someone had advised them to soft-pedal stuff like that around me because it might upset their poor traumatized daughter in her delicate condition. Actually, it was more upsetting to me to have them walking around on eggshells, trying not to say the wrong thing or do anything that might set me off. It made me feel fragile, like a piece of antique china locked up in a cupboard.

I finally realized I had to do something. I knocked on the door of their room one night. I just knew they were up and talking about me. Sure enough, when they told me to come on in, I could hear that little hesitation in their voices that made me certain they'd been talking about poor Molly.

I sat down on the edge of the bed, then leaned over and put my head on my father's shoulder.

"Daddy," I said, "tell me a story."

"I don't know," my father said. My mom bit her lip.

I sat up and looked first at him and then at Mom.

"Listen," I said, "I'm still Molly. Remember me? I need to hear a story. And make it a scary one, okay?"

I guess the tone of my voice must have been a little stronger than I intended because both my parents raised their eyebrows. Then my mother laughed.

"She's baa-aack," my father said. And then he told me a story that was so scary I asked my parents if I could sleep with them that night. All three of us fell asleep with a smile on our face.

The thing about scary stories, you see, is that they're reassuring. At least they are for me. Like I said before, life really is dangerous. There truly are things for people to be afraid of—if not giant cannibals in the forest, then other people who can be just as dangerous. The stories have always helped me deal with my fears. Remember, the scariest monster is the one you don't see. After that big mechanical shark in *Jaws* finally comes to the surface and starts chomping on the boat, it is nowhere near as terrifying as it was at the start of the movie, when you just heard that music and then saw a swirl of blood and one or two leftover body parts sinking to the bottom. So the stories help me see my fears and then deal with them. Once Dad started telling stories again, we really did get back to normal.

Coming to this conference with my parents is yet another way of their letting me know they think I'm ready to deal with the outside world—or at least the microcosm that is Mohonk. This huge resort hotel has more than seven hundred employees. Some of them live in New Paltz and the other little communities around Mohonk, but a lot of them stay right here on the premises in the dormitory for workers.

I can understand why. The main road that leads up to the Mohonk Mountain House is winding and long. I can't imagine what it was like building it. In some spots the road is narrow and right next to the edge of the cliffs, which have long drop-offs. It must take a lot of maintenance to keep the road open in winter or to repair it when there are rock slides. I saw some big machines—a bulldozer, a front-end loader, and a dump truck—parked in a pull-off area where the road started winding around after we passed the gatehouse.

"How'd you like to drive that baby?" my dad said to me, pointing at the bulldozer with his chin as we slowly passed it.

"I'd love it," I said.

I wasn't kidding. Dad operated machinery like that during the summers when he was working his way through college. He's never lost his love for those things and keeps little yellow model construction vehicles of all kinds on a shelf by his desk. He's remained friends with some of the men he worked with back then and visits them now and then on their jobs. I must have inherited that "knock things down, build things up" gene, as my mom calls it, from my father.

I've gone along with him on some of those jaunts. It is usually a real hands-on visit, because Dad always has to climb up into the cab of whatever new behemoth they've got and try the controls. I don't know how many times I've sat on his lap, my own yellow hardhat on my head, with my hands on his as he drove a front-end loader or dozer, or operated a crane. Since I've gotten older, I've even been allowed to work the controls myself at times. Nowadays there are women on some sites operating those big machines.

On the drive up here I didn't notice anyone using the bulldozer or loader. They probably wouldn't have been left unguarded like that if they hadn't been on this side of the gatehouse, secure. The gatehouse marks the start of the private Mohonk road. It's the only official way in. This main road ends at a loop, with the Mountain House at the far end of it. There's a smaller, secondary road called Mossy Brook Road that swings off that loop, but it is so little, it makes the narrow main road look like a superhighway.

Everyone who comes up to the Mountain House has to check in at the Mohonk Mountain House gate just like we did our first day. You have to be an employee with ID, or your name has to be on the guest list, or you have to pay a fee to come up for the day or to get lunch or dinner. You have to either park your car in a big lot near the gatehouse and take the shuttle bus up or drive your car the remaining two miles to where the valets park it for you.

That is one reason why my dad's convention is being held here, because it is so organized and safe and secure. It is what they call a "controlled environment."

But lots of events do take place here. Dad's

conference isn't the only thing going on. At Mohonk this weekend they are also celebrating the Day of the Dead, which is a Mexican festival, along with Halloween. Halloween, as every kid knows, is on October 31. Its name comes, as a lot of kids *don't* know, from the eve of All Hallows, a time to celebrate all the Christian saints. (Forgive me, but you are now dealing with Molly the information junkie, who you should never ever dare to take on in a game of Trivial Pursuit.)

The Day of the Dead is actually the two days right after Halloween, November 1 and 2. It is an old indigenous celebration. The Aztecs celebrated it around the end of what we call the month of July. It was presided over by Mictecacihuatl, the "Lady of the Dead," who was a powerful, benevolent being who loved little children and even acted as their protector, a sort of messenger from the ancestors, who were always watching over their descendants. But the priests who arrived with the Spanish conquistadors didn't appreciate that the local people followed the old ways. They wanted them to honor just the Christian saints. They tried to wipe out the holiday, but the Indians wouldn't give it up. So the Spanish moved it to the beginning of November to coincide with El Día de Todos Santos, the Day of All Saints or All Saints' Day, as well as All Souls' Day.

The Day of the Dead is huge in Mexico, where life and death are seen in a different way than they are in most of the United States. People go to cemeteries to honor their dead relatives. There are fireworks and people dress up in devil masks and costumes to look like skeletons. They even give kids candy shaped like little skulls. Because there are so many Mexican Americans in the United States, it has been popular in the American Southwest, too. It's a new idea having a Day of the Dead here at the hotel, almost two thousand miles from Mexico. The poster I read about it says that it is Mohonk Mountain House's way of "continuing to celebrate the multicultural tapestry that is the United States today." Whatever.

Some people would say that my parents were either cruel or crazy to take a kid who'd experienced the kind of trauma I did to a place where they were celebrating not just Halloween but also the Day of the Dead. Not just one event focusing on ghosts and death but two. Practically child abuse. But I think it's great. My parents always told me that you have to face your fears. If you turn away from them, they can just sneak up and grab you from behind. The fact that my parents would actually take me to something like this after all we went through with Skeleton Man really shows how much they believe I have gotten back to normal.

Normal, though, doesn't necessarily mean safe.

Like right now.

They are showing a movie tonight here at the hotel, right after the music is done. I've been feeling antsy all day, actually ever since dinner last night. I guess I need to get out of the room. It's a full hour till the concert starts, so I've decided to poke around the hotel. Dad has an evening meeting and won't be able to go to the concert, although he'll join us in time for the film.

Mom has told me she'll meet me at the concert. Rather than head straight there, I decided to go upstairs and explore the wing I haven't seen yet. So here I am walking this long dark corridor alone.

There's this sound that your feet make on a wooden floor when no one else is walking on it but you, like the floor is talking to you in a different language. You don't know how to speak that language, but you can comprehend it the same way you understand the growling of a big animal that's out there just beyond the light of your fire.

Kuhh-reeeaak. Kuhh-reeeaak.

Walking slower just makes it worse. This hallway seems to go on forever. I try walking faster. I'm humming "A Little Bit of Luck" under my breath to the beat of my footsteps, but not the whole song, because I don't know it. Just this one refrain, which shows how nervous I am making myself.

> *With a little bit,*
> *with a little bit,*
>
> *with a little bit of luck*
> *I won't get caught.*

Caught by what? This is dumb. I stop humming. Immediately I start to notice that the sound of my footsteps is getting louder. Each footfall seems to be echoing. Am I hearing someone else's feet hitting just half a step after mine? I stop and listen, but I don't hear anything. I pretend to take a step, then whirl around to look behind me. There's nothing there but the empty hall and the old black-and-white photos hanging along the walls. Not even a shadow. Every door is closed. Nothing to be afraid of.

But I start running anyway. Sometimes seeing nothing is just as ominous as seeing something. I don't know if that sounds crazy, but right now it makes sense to me. I find a stairway and I thud down it, and all of a sudden I'm not alone at all. Just half a flight below me I see people walking along, talking and acting normal. One or two of them are turning to look up at the wild-eyed teenager descending the stairs like a deer stampeding down a slope away from a mountain lion.

"Take it easy, honey," I hear a woman say. She's got hold of my arm—not so hard that it hurts, but firm enough to have stopped my headlong progress. It takes me a second to realize that she's just saved me from running into her and sending both of us rolling down the stairs. She must be a maid, because she is wearing one of the hotel's uniforms. The towels she dropped when she grabbed me are at her feet. She is also holding a big red potted chrysanthemum in her other arm. Its heady smell is all around us.

"I'm sorry," I say. "I just . . ." Just what? I don't know.

"S'all right, honey," the woman says. She has some kind of accent, maybe Central American. She looks up at me as she says this, because she is not at all tall, no more than five feet, but she looks compact and strong. Her face is even a little browner than my dad's and I find myself wondering how much Indian blood she has. Her ID tag tells me her name is Corazón.

"You all right?" she says. Her voice is soft, confidential.

I nod.

She lets go of my arm to set the chrysanthemum down on the landing. Then she picks up the towels, places them on a little seat built into the stairwell behind her, and straightens out my sweater, which has gotten twisted around. Her touch is as reassuring as my mom's.

"Thanks," I say.

Corazón smiles. She looks at my face closely and then nods in recognition. "Indio," she says. It's not a question.

"I'm Mohawk."

Corazón smiles at me again, one of those smiles that just lights up a face. She puts her right hand on her heart.

"Mayan," she says.

I'm not sure when we sat down, but we're sitting together now, as if we are old friends. I hope I'm not getting her into trouble because she's supposed to be working, but I'm really glad that she's here with me. I look over at the towels she was carrying.

"S'all right," Corazón says again. "My shift is just over. I take these down, drop them off, go home. It is my time now."

I'm feeling a lot saner now. Sane enough to be embarrassed. "I'm sorry," I say. "I don't know what made me do that."

Corazón leans over toward me and looks into my

eyes. Her own eyes are dark, just like mine. Her face is also just as smooth and unlined as mine, but I'm sure she is older than me. Not as old as my mom, but she has to be at least twenty.

"This place," she says. She doesn't say it as if she is afraid or unhappy about being here. It's more like she is just making an observation. "Sometimes when I walk up there, I think I am not alone. You maybe felt like somebody was looking at you?"

"That's it," I say. "That's exactly it."

"*Los muertos,*" Corazón says. "The dead are watching."

DOWN THE HALLWAY

CORAZÓN IS WAVING AT me from the doorway, not with her whole hand but with her fingers in a fluttery gesture that makes me think of a butterfly. She's smiling as she waves and then she touches her heart. I smile back and tap my own chest with the fingers of my right hand. I feel such a connection to her.

Part of it is her being Indian, like me. Just from our short talk, too, I can tell that she understands things I can't talk to a lot of people about. Things that some people would call being foolish or superstitious. Things like being guided by your dreams.

"My great-great-grandfather," she had told me in a soft, sure voice that had only a little bit of a Spanish accent. "His name was Chan K'in. That means 'Little Sun' or 'Little Prophet.' He was over 130 years old when he passed away a few years ago. We little ones would sit at his feet around the fire at night and he would tell stories. Then every morning he would ask us what we had dreamed about. He would listen closely to our dreams and help us understand the messages those dreams brought to us. He taught me how to interpret dream messages."

So I told her about the rabbit and about Skeleton Man. Just the short version. But it still took twenty minutes.

When I finished my story, Corazón shivered as if she had just felt a cold breeze. Then she reached out one hand and tapped it lightly on the wood bench where we were sitting. I understood that gesture. You knock on wood when you think something bad may be about to happen. It's a way of summoning good to come and protect you. She was silent for a while before she spoke again.

"I think my great–great-grandfather might have said your rabbit was speaking with an ancestor's voice. He was watching over you in the same way that our Lady of the Dead always watches out for our children. Do you know about the one the Azteca call Mictecacihuatl?"

"A little," I replied. That brought a smile to Corazón's face.

"I think you have *mucho fortuna*," she said. "Much fortune."

"I think so too," I replied.

I looked at my watch. I had that feeling you get when a story has just ended and you find yourself back in the "real" world again, and you wonder how much time has passed. This time it was more than I'd realized.

"Oh my gosh," I said. "It's almost time for the concert. I have to meet my mom."

Corazón picked up her towels, put them under one arm, and stood. "Come," she said, holding out her hand to me. "I know the quickest way to get there."

"What a lovely young woman," Mom says as Corazón disappears around the corner. "It was very nice of her to help you find your way here after you got turned around. This is a big place and those long hallways can be confusing."

More than just confusing, I think. But I am not going to mention to Mom how freaked out I was before I ran into Corazón . . . or how I almost ran over her.

Mom had asked Corazón if she could stay and listen to the music with us, but Corazón shook her head and said something in Spanish that I didn't catch. But my mother, who speaks not just Mohawk and English—like my dad and me—but also three or four other languages, nodded and answered something back to her in Spanish that made Corazón put her hand over her mouth and giggle.

I wait until Corazón is out of sight and turn to my mom.

"What did she say?" I demand. Typical Molly.

I always have to know everything that is going on.

"Just a proverb, honey. I'll tell you later. The music's about to start. I think you're going to like this."

By the time the evening concert is over, an hour later, I'm in total agreement with my mother. In fact, I didn't just like it, I loved it. I even danced with my mom to a couple of the square dance tunes they played. Contrary to what she and Dad had told me, there were *not* lots of kids my age at the dance. But that was okay. Also, one member of Quickstep was a cute guy who probably wasn't much older than me. He looked shy, but I am sure he smiled at me once or twice. It made me feel like he was playing just for me. He had a very cool name, too—Cedar, just like the tree.

"I hope we can see that group again sometime," I say to Mom as we walk toward the movie. I am totally at ease now and there is nothing at all scary about the corridor that was so creepy when I was walking it on my own.

"Did you see that boy who was playing the fiddle?" she says.

"Mom!" I hate it when she seems to read my mind like this. I stop and stare at her. "I was talking about the group, not just that one guy. What do you mean?"

"I just meant," she says, a little smile on her lips, "that he seemed very talented, even though he was so young."

"Oh," I say, my face reddening. "Yes, I guess so."

Then I smile like my mom is smiling. Maybe everything is going to be all right after all. We meet up with my dad and I manage to keep thinking that way all through the movie. But as we are walking back, I find myself a few steps behind my parents. I stop to look at one of the old photos on the wall, and suddenly I get that feeling again. I'm being watched. I spin around to look down the hall behind me. For just a second I think I see someone, a tall, thin person with a pale face fading back into a doorway. I take one step in that direction, then another.

"Molly."

My mom's voice brings me out of my trance. I turn around and realize that I have walked back the whole length of the hall. My hand is holding the knob of the door through which I thought I saw that tall, pale shape disappear.

I jerk my hand back like it's been burned. I don't want to open this door. A shiver goes down my spine as I turn and head back toward my mother, who's holding out her hand to me, a questioning look on her face. I force myself to walk to her, even though I want to run. I manage to force a smile back onto my face.

There's nothing wrong, I tell myself.

But the knot in my stomach is as hard as a fist. Was my imagination going crazy on me or had I really seen someone disappear through that door? I am afraid to think that I know the answer—and who might be waiting on the other side.

THE LOOKOUT

T HE NEXT MORNING IT is sunny when I wake
up. At first that seems strange, because I
feel as if I was just in a very dark, unpleas-
ant place, and this room is the opposite of that. I feel
as if there are cobwebs on my face, and I wipe my
eyes. I know I was having a bad dream, but this time
I can't quite remember what it was. Or maybe I just
don't want to remember.

I get up and let the sunshine touch my face. A

little breeze is coming through the open window. There's still that taste in the air that you get in fall when the light outside is so clear that it seems to vibrate and it is as warm as some summer days. I can tell it's a fragile warmth. It might blow away as quickly as the seeds on a dandelion, but it makes me want to go outside and walk. I need to do something like stroll through a garden and this is the best place to do that.

"I'm going for a walk," I say, looking into my parents' room after getting ready.

"Want me to come along?" my mom asks.

There's a breakfast tray with coffee and juice and pastries in front of her and my father. I know she's not ready yet to go out. She'd probably like to have some time alone with Dad, who doesn't have to leave for his next seminar for another two hours. But she's ready to come with me if I need company. The thought of the two of them sitting together and having breakfast makes me feel warm and secure. It's like sunshine on my face.

"It's okay," I say. "I'd just like to walk by myself and check out the summerhouses. I am going to try

189

to sit in every single one."

That makes my dad laugh. He knows I'll try to do it, even though there are over a hundred summerhouses here at Mohonk. They even sell a little booklet in the gift shop called *The Summerhouses of Mohonk*. They aren't like gazebos, which are intricate and planned. The summerhouses of Mohonk are rustic. Some are nothing more than a bench with a roof, and every one is different. A lot of them are made of dark, old, twisting cedar logs with the bark still on them. They're like grandparents, just waiting for you to climb up onto their laps.

And that's what I do. I sit in each one that I find, lean back, feel how it is to be there, look out at the view it commands, give a contented sigh, and then head to the next one.

Every single summerhouse is placed so it has a different scenic view. I said there were over a hundred, but no one knows for sure how many there are. The earliest inventory was done in 1917 when they listed 155 summerhouses. Nowadays they claim there are 125. Most have a brass tag with a four-digit number that is entered into the Mohonk computer base. But there may still be forgotten ones tucked off in the woods. Some of them are way down winding paths and others are perched up on the edges of cliffs, with wooden bridges and stairs leading to them. The one on Sentinel Rock overlooks the lake and the whole Mountain House. The best ones, though, as far as I'm concerned, overlook the flower gardens. Although most of the flowers are gone now, you can see how beautiful this place must be when they are in bloom.

"House number twenty-eight," I say to myself.

The sun is still shining in my face as I settle down on the cedar bench. A bent wood roof with rough shingles hangs over it, covered by a vine of some kind that has been trained over the top. At its base that vine is as thick as my waist, and I wonder how old it is. My eyes follow it as it climbs from the ground toward the roof, then something in the distance catches my eye.

I'm looking out at one of the wooded ridges that rise above the gardens. It is at least two hundred yards away and a hundred feet higher in elevation than me. There's another summerhouse there, one that I hadn't noticed before. Even with the leaves off the trees, it is hard to see it, tucked away up there on the lookout. But it's not the summerhouse that has caught my eye—rather, a flash of light from inside it. It's the kind of flash of light when the sun hits a mirror or something made of glass.

I raise up my hand to shade my eyes. Another flash of light comes from inside that summerhouse on the highest slope. And even though it is so far away, I am certain about what I'm seeing. It's a pair of binoculars and they are pointing right at me. I can just barely make out the pale head and gloved hands of the person holding them. That person is wearing a hat, and he's so far away I can't really see his face, but something tells me that it's a man. While I'm staring, those binoculars are slowly pulled back. All I can see now is the shadowy opening of the summerhouse.

I wait. For some reason, my heart is thumping in my chest, even though there's no reason to get upset about somebody with binoculars. People carry them around here all the time. It's the season when hawks migrate. Just yesterday there was a whole gaggle of bird-watchers on the ridge, all staring up through their spotting scopes and binoculars at a huge flock of broad-winged hawks sweeping by, following the Shawangunk Ridge toward the south.

Staring up. That's it. You don't look down to see hawks, you look up into the sky. There's still no motion from the summerhouse on the ridge. The way the trees grow around it I can see only the front from where I'm sitting. I have to go there. Half of my brain says I'm being foolish, that there's nothing to be afraid of. The other half says I'm being fool-hardy. Why am I taking the path that leads up to that lookout? How do I know there's not something dangerous up there just waiting for me?

I'm breathing hard by the time I reach the sum-merhouse on the ridge. I can see now that it is balanced right on top of a huge, flat boulder. There's no one here. I look around. No sign of anyone on the gravel path leading down in either direction. Was I just imagining that I saw someone?

I sit down on the bench and look down. There's a perfect view of not just the garden but also the Mountain House itself. I spot the summerhouse where I had been sitting. I have to lean out and to the right to get a clear view of it. As I do so, I put my hand on the bench. My palm finds something small and round, something that I hadn't noticed when I sat down. When I see what it is, a chill shivers down my back and I almost drop what I'm holding—a small, perfectly molded white candy skull.

9

SKULLS

I STILL HAVE THE candy skull in my hand. But now I'm feeling like a jerk. I sprinted all the way back to the Mountain House in a panic, thumped up the steps, burst through the door of the Lake Lounge, and what did I see? The tables are awash with marigolds and chrysanthemums. And in the midst of those flowers are bowls half-filled with candy skulls just like mine. The candy skulls are just part of the whole Day of the Dead theme.

Some of them look like human skulls and some are like the skulls of animals. Boys and girls are wandering around with their parents, candy skulls in their hands—or their mouths. Some kid was probably walking on that path, sat down in the summerhouse, and just left the skull up there by accident. Nothing sinister. Just kids and candy.

The one I have in my hand has gotten sticky from the sweat in my palm. It's starting to dissolve, just like the panic that had gripped me so hard that I felt as if I had been hit in the stomach.

Get a grip, girl, I tell myself. I pick up a paper napkin, wrap my no longer ominous piece of candy in it, and drop it into a wastebasket. Then I wipe my hand clean. I won't mention this to my parents. I'll just let them think I had a great walk. No attack of absolute gut-wrenching terror. It was just a carefree afternoon for me, sitting in one summerhouse after another, enjoying the quiet beauty and feeling that all was right with the world.

I head back to my room, say hi to my parents, and then slump into the chair by the window and pick up my book for a bit of leisurely reading. Only I can't concentrate on anything. I can't shake this eerie feeling that something just isn't right.

No. Everything is fine. Just fine.

"Time for dinner, honey," Mom announces after a while. "Are you ready?"

My parents and I get a table near the windows in the big semi-circular dining room with the high ceiling and wooden beams. Our table would normally be a great place to sit because you can look way out over the valleys and see the far-off lights of houses and the shadowy hills in the twilight. But this evening all I can see is mist. I can't even see the trees and bushes on the lawn right below. I'm feeling closed in, trapped. I wish I could see through that mist, and see if anything was out there. Then I start thinking about what I might see, what I don't want to see. I squirm in my seat.

"Molly," Dad says, "are you okay?"

He and Mom are looking right at me. I almost give them one of those "Oh, I'm fine" replies. I don't want to worry them needlessly, after everything we've gone through. But my mouth reacts before my brain can stop it.

"No," I say. "I'm not." For some reason, that actually makes me feel a little better.

"Why, honey?" Mom asks. But something about the way she asks it tells me that she already has a good idea.

"I feel," I say, balling my napkin up between my palms, "like I'm being watched by . . . somebody."

I wait for them to reassure me, to tell me I am being foolish. But they don't. Instead, my mother and father exchange a long look, and finally my father nods.

"I know," Dad says. "I've been feeling the same way. There's something not quite right lately. I keep telling myself that I'm being foolish, but I still have bad dreams about what happened to us. I don't see . . . him . . . in my dreams, but I can feel him watching us. Then, the next thing I know, my hands are tied and you and Mom are in danger and I can't get free to save you."

My mouth drops open and I stare at my father. I've never thought about how he and Mom were affected by what happened to us. All I've been able to think about are my own feelings. But they were in just as much danger as I was. And my dad, who I used to think was big and strong and smart enough to defeat any monster in the world, had been helpless.

"They never found his body," I say. I'm amazed at how calm and logical my voice sounds.

"I know," Dad replies.

"Why would he come after us?"

My mom is the one who answers that. "Because we got away," she says. "Because we got away."

"I feel," I say, pausing for a moment and then just saying it, "I feel as if he's here somewhere. Am I crazy?"

I look at my parents closely. I think what I really want is for them to tell me there is nothing to fear, that we are totally safe now and forever. But that is not what they do.

"You're not crazy," Mom says.

"No, you are not," Dad agrees, his voice slow and careful. "I feel as if . . . he . . . is here, too."

"Sk . . . Sk . . . ," I say, trying to speak the name that none of us have wanted to ever hear again.

"Skeleton Man," Mom says.

WALKING THE FIELD

ONE THING THAT SCARY movies never really focus on is all the times when nothing happens. They make it seem as if one frightening thing always happens right after another without any letup. But life isn't like that. Sometimes, for long stretches of time, nothing at all happens. You just find yourself waiting, and waiting, and not really knowing what is going to happen or when.

And that is how it has been for the rest

of the day, after Mom and Dad and I had our conversation about Skeleton Man. We talked it over and came to what we thought were good decisions.

"Should we call the police?" I asked.

"No, I don't think so," Mom said.

Dad nodded. "All we have are suspicions, Molly girl. You *think* you saw something. And Mom and I both have that kind of sixth-sense tingle at the back of our neck. The kind of feeling which my gramma said meant something was looking your way that you didn't want to meet. And you've got your dreams. But it doesn't mean as much as a hill of beans to the authorities. We'd have to have some solid evidence. Something you could sink your teeth into."

"More than a candy skull?" I said.

It wasn't that funny, but I giggled as I said it and then both Dad and Mom were laughing. It released the tension we were all sensing and made us feel so much better. We could still laugh and be together. Everything could still turn out all right.

We came up with sort of a plan. A big part of it was to all be on our guard. I would stay close to either Mom or Dad the rest of the time we were here. We wouldn't leave Mohonk until the conference was over, because we couldn't be sure that we really were in danger. No foolish risks, though. No shopping trip down to New Paltz. No more of my solo hikes along the trails or down darkened corridors.

But we wouldn't act like timid little mice who suspect they are being stalked by a cat. If we just cut and ran every time we got worried, our lives wouldn't belong to us anymore. We'd never be at peace if all we did was try to escape. And besides, we would be here only two more days. Not only that, this was such a special, beautiful place. If we let our fear of something that might or might not happen prevent us from enjoying it, then Skeleton Man really would have won.

One thing that is different now is that I have a cell phone. After all that happened, when it was over, Dad gave me one to keep with me wherever I go.

"Indian telepathy is okay," he said, "but this way I can hear your voice when you need to talk to me."

We both chuckled about that reference to my sixth sense. In the old, old days, some of our elders say, people could really communicate with each other mind-to-mind. A cell phone is a pretty good substitute for that legendary kind of communication.

Having my little phone in my pocket all the time has made me feel more secure. Mom has one, too. So we can make an emergency call to one another or to the authorities at any time. And that is part of our plan, too. If anyone sees or experiences anything out of the ordinary, anything threatening, we can just flip out our phone, hit the button, and communicate. If we learn something tangible, if we really do see Skeleton Man, then we can call the police.

There is another side to our plan. If we don't act all spooked and if Skeleton Man is really here, really watching us, maybe he'll make some kind of mistake. He has underestimated us before, and he might again. So we planned to do fun things—especially things where there would be a lot of people around, like concerts or the afternoon tea, or the Day of the

Dead party planned for the next night.

The rest of that evening after dinner the three of us felt so much better, because we had a plan, that the time just whizzed by. We went to bed, and even though we had concluded there was a real chance that our lives were in danger, we had a good night's sleep. We got up and ate breakfast. Dad went to his meetings while Mom and I took a walk together. Then we sat around and read. I did my reading in the window seat where I could look out at the lake and the cliffs across the way, and I finished *Briar Rose*. Mom tried to get through the latest historical novel she was reading, but every time I looked up she would either just be staring off into space or be looking over at me. She didn't really relax until we met Dad for lunch.

"Quiet morning, girls?" he asked.

"Unh-huh," I said.

Mom just nodded, and she squeezed Dad's hand under the table most of the time we were eating. Then Mom and I went to an early afternoon chamber music concert in the Lake Lounge.

To the outside world, we've been acting as if we

don't have a care in the world, but it's just an act. If we are being watched, we don't want to make it look like we're suspicious.

And now it is time for us to do part of what we'd planned. Mom pulls out the *Historical Features of the Mountain House* booklet that we just bought at the gift shop.

"Well, we have a couple of hours before afternoon tea. Shall we do that self-guided tour, honey?" she asks.

She sounds like she is reading bad dialogue from a second-rate movie. That is one problem with having made a plan. Spontaneity is hard to fake. And my response to her, despite myself, is just as bright and stiff.

"Sure, Mom, that sounds like a great idea."

We take a look at the map inside the booklet. We actually have already spent time studying it. It shows the five huge interconnected wings that make up the Mountain House: Rock Building, Stone Building, Central Building, Grove Building, and the Kitchen and Dining Room Building.

"Oh," Mom says, with the inflection of a bad

high school understudy trying to remember her lines now that the lead actress has come down with the flu, "there's our friend. *¿Cómo está usted?*"

"*Bien, gracias,*" Corazón answers. Thankfully, her voice is not at all strained. It helps Mom and me to relax. What helps even more is when, as she gives each of us a hug, she whispers, "Don't worry" in our ears.

Our accidental meeting is no accident. After dinner we had found Corazón and asked her to help us. So she's arranged to have this afternoon off to walk the corridors with us. Corazón, who has worked here for almost a year, is going to point out things that most tourists would not care about or need to know.

The three of us just look like friends strolling along, talking and laughing. But inside, Mom and I are not just being tourists. We're doing what my dad used to do when he was a star lacrosse player. Before each match he would walk the field to familiarize himself with every inch of the place where the game would be played.

And as we do this, as Corazón whispers things

to us like where keys are kept and what the hidden ways are in this huge old maze of a place, that feeling from yesterday comes back again. It's like walking into a darkened room, right into a spiderweb that you don't see until it brushes across your face and sticks there.

11

SNOW

W E'VE MADE IT THROUGH the day. Dad
and Mom and I are sitting at our
favorite table by the window. Noth-
ing strange has happened except for the snow. A
freak storm has swept in from the west and is dump-
ing more snow than I have ever seen in October.
From what the forecasters say, it is falling mostly
here in the mountains. Down in the valley below,
there is hardly any snow at all, and in some cases

there is just cold rain.

Snow. All kinds of thoughts are going through my head. Memories of making snowballs, and snow angels and snowmen, and forts. Up on the Rez, snow always means it is time to lay down boards on the back lawn and turn on the hose to make an instant hockey rink. Even though I didn't grow up on the Rez, Dad has made sure I've always had my own skates, and I can swing a stick as well as any boy. When we go up there in the winter, I have my skates and pads, ready to take on my cousins in one of our knock-'em-down, drag-'em-out pick-up games. Lots of scoring and bloody noses. I'm good enough so that I am usually one of the first three or four picked for a side. There's such a feeling of free-dom when you can just glide over the ice as if you are flying—and then bodycheck someone so that he flies head over heels into one of the snowdrifts around the rink and steal the puck from him.

There are also Mohawk stories involving snow. Terrible giants sometimes show up in the stories my dad tells. Their skins and their hearts are made of ice and they have no human feelings, just a hunger that can never be satisfied.

The snow swirls across the window. This is ice-giant weather for sure. The waiter stops by our table.

"I know you folks said you weren't planning on going anywhere," he says, "but I thought I should let you know that this storm has gotten pretty bad." He looks out the window and shakes his head. "We don't get anything like this in the Dominican Republic. Anyhow, they've closed the road down the mountain. Nobody will be getting out of here tonight."

Nobody will be getting out of here. Those few innocent words send a chill down my back.

While we wait for our food to come, we don't talk. Instead, Dad and Mom and I just look out the window at the swirling patterns of snow. It is hard to see any shapes beyond the branches of the nearest trees. They still have autumn leaves and the snow is making their branches bend dangerously low to the ground, strained to the point of breaking. Weather like this knocks down not just branches but also power lines and phone lines and then you are cut off from the outside world. I don't like the thought of that.

There could be almost anything out there hidden by that snow. There could be a huge hairy elephant, just like the one in that story by Rafe Martin called *Will's Mammoth*. That used to be my favorite picture book when I was little. Or there could be a whole army of ice giants creeping up on us through the howling storm. I try to imagine them out there, those huge monsters from the old tales. Thinking of mammoths and ice giants is a lot safer than thinking about the one real monster that I escaped from. Imaginary monsters are nowhere near as scary. And the stories always end with you sitting safe and warm at home or around the fire in the longhouse.

But my thoughts won't stay in that safe, fanciful place. Anything could be hidden by that snow. Anything.

12

MASKS

THE DAY OF THE Dead party is being held in the Lake Lounge tonight. We have decided to be totally minimalist in what we're wearing. No full-face masks hide our features. Just those little Lone Ranger masks. No weird alien outfits with extra limbs. We want to be able to see and recognize one another when we are in the crowd of people. Dad is dressed as a Mohawk high-steel construction worker. That was easy for him.

He had thought ahead when he was packing and brought along his old work clothes, from his boots and coveralls to the hardhat with an eagle painted on it. He even has a big spanner wrench stuck in his belt.

Mom and I aren't really wearing costumes. We never use the word *costume* to describe traditional clothing. What we have on is just that, the traditional buckskin dresses with beautiful beadwork that we wear to powwows. We hear appreciative remarks from people as we sweep by. The only risk is that someone will think Mom and I are supposed to be dressed as Pocahontas and her mother. No way. I am Molly Brant, warrior woman. And Mom is dressed as Jigonsaseh, the woman who helped the Peacemaker and Hiawatha found the great Iroquois League of Peace by being the first person to speak in favor of their idea.

The clothing we're wearing is not just beautiful. It is comfortable and practical, too. You can run in a buckskin dress. It doesn't hold you back and restrict you like long dresses with petticoats and tight cinched-in waists. I see some of the girls going down the hall dressed in Cinderella costumes. If they got knocked over, it would be as hard for them to get up as it is for a turtle to get off its back.

Corazón is going to be here at the party, working. I close my eyes to imagine how she might look in traditional garb and I suddenly see her in my mind's eye. She's wearing a calf-length white dress decorated with beautiful embroidery in all the colors of the rainbow. A jaguar-skin robe is draped over her shoulders and in one hand is either a long knife or a short spear. She wears a crown made of colorful parrot feathers and long quetzal plumes. An intricate necklace made of gold hangs around her neck, jangling bracelets of gold and silver are on her wrists and ankles, and anklets of jaguar skin rest above her bare feet. There's a glow about her as if she has been lit by some inner light. I don't know what traditional Mayan dress looks like, so I'm not sure where this picture in my mind has just come from. It puzzles me a little bit. What puzzles me even more is why that mental image of her seems to grow and come into clearer focus, so clear that I can see the gold shapes that are linked together in her bracelets and anklets and necklace, and I know what they really are. Each link is a tiny gold skull. And I recognize who she is. The Lady of the Dead.

Sí, I am the Lady, a voice whispers in my head. *I greet you, my little sister.*

I open my eyes and blink. That vision of Corazón is gone and I see her coming down the hallway toward us. Her work clothing is not at all exotic. She has on sensible white tennis shoes and a plain uniform dress, its only decoration the embroidered Mohonk Mountain House logo. Its gray color indicates that she is a member of the serving staff.

The clothes worn by the employees here have different colors and designs according to the different jobs they do. When we first arrived and Dad gave our car keys to the valet he had joked about that with the young man in the green shirt who took our car and the older man in the dark brown shirt who was clearly the younger man's supervisor. "If I wore a purple shirt," Dad said, "would that make me the king?" I guess that doesn't sound so funny when I tell it, but the way my dad said it and the smile he gave them made everyone chuckle.

Corazón has obviously come out to greet us. We've just passed the Winter Lounge and the gift shop and have not yet made the left-hand turn that brings us to the Lake Lounge. We can hear the sound of music being played rather loudly.

"*Buenas noches*," Corazón says. Then she looks back over her shoulder. "It is very crowded in there," she says in a softer voice, "but I have not seen anyone who might be that person you are worried about. Even a costume cannot hide a man's height."

Dad nods. We have told Corazón about the man who abducted them and pretended to be my uncle. We described him as best we could, even though all three of us realized as we did so that it was hard to have a clear image of what he really looked like in our minds. And that is strange because we all have a good memory for faces. All we could remember was that he was far from being a young man, though he didn't move as if he were elderly. He had a kind of energy about him that was intense. He was tall, tall enough to have been a basketball player, with long thin arms and legs and very big hands. There was something about him that looked Indian, but it was hard to define, as hard as it was to describe his features except to say that they were bony and skull-like.

Corazón is holding a serving tray out to us with small loaves of bread on it.

"Take one," she says, "and bite into it. But do not bite hard, *sí*?"

Even though we ate only an hour ago, those little loaves look good to me. They are still warm from the oven. I bite into one and my teeth strike something. I reach into my mouth and pull it out. It is a small white plastic skeleton.

13

DARKNESS

AD AND MOM AND I are in the Lake Lounge now. Just as Corazón said, it is packed with people. Except for the servers, everyone is in costume, both grown-ups and kids. Some are just wearing premolded masks that cover their heads. After all these years, it seems, Richard Nixon is still as popular as Dracula or the Wolf Man or Jason from *Friday the 13th*. But others are wearing really elaborate costumes. Because this is a blend of Halloween and the Mexican Day of the Dead, there are zombies and Zorros, witches and Spanish señoritas, robots and banditos. There's been some research done. I see someone wearing a sign around her neck identifying her as La Llorona, the wailing woman of Mexican folklore. A handsome-looking man in conquistador garb and a woman whose knee-length dark hair has to be a wig are telling everyone within earshot that they are Hernando Cortés and La Malinche, the Indian woman who was his interpreter and ally during the conquest of Mexico.

I'm finding it all kind of amusing and confusing at the same time. In part that is because I am trying to stick like glue to my dad's side and not let go of my mother's hand. It is also because, like my parents, I keep scanning the crowd for a man who is a head taller than everyone else. And there's a third reason for my feeling of disquiet.

It's not what you think, though. It is not that little skeleton I found in my piece of bread. No, that wasn't a mean trick played on me by Corazón. That special bread was what Mexican people call *pan de muerto*, or the bread of the dead. It is considered to be good luck to be the one who bites into the small toy skeleton hidden inside the loaf. The fact that the little loaves taken by my mother and father had nothing in them was a sign of how lucky I had been in choosing that piece. That little plastic skeleton was in my pocket now.

The reason I am feeling uneasy is hard to explain. I guess it started when I saw the first person in a skeleton costume. It wasn't *him*. That person was way too short and the costume was just a body suit with skeletal bones painted on it. But it gave me a start.

I look back over my shoulder and catch the eye of Corazón, who has been moving about the room with her serving tray. She is acting as another set of eyes for us, helping us keep watch. She smiles and then shakes her head. She hasn't seen anything for us to worry about. At least not yet. Still, I feel a sudden cold chill, as if a little of the early winter wind has just blown across my neck.

A feeling is growing inside me that something is

very wrong, but I don't know what it is. I turn to look out the window. Spotlights are shining on the new snow and everything is almost as clear as day. That's encouraging. I'm not usually afraid of the dark, but tonight I don't want to look out and see nothing but darkness, a darkness that might hide something that is coming closer with every hidden step. I'm glad it is brightly lit inside this room. Bright enough for me to see anything or anyone that might be a danger to us.

What a crazy thought. There's no reason for me to be so uptight. But I don't let go of my mom's hand and I keep looking around. Then I see something that seems out of place—a person across the room, sitting in a chair near one of the doors that leads out onto the porch. His costume is weird. I can't tell what he is supposed to be. He's wearing a heavy coat, and a ski mask is covering most of his head. But he also has some kind of contraption on top of his head that looks like really complicated binoculars. He slowly lifts a long hand up to brush snow off his shoulder. He's just come in from outside. It must have been when he slipped into the room that I felt that cold breeze on my neck. He looks in my direction, then reaches that long hand up to pull those binoculars down over his eyes like goggles. Is he supposed to be dressed as a space alien?

I squeeze my mom's hand harder, pulling on it to turn her around to see what I'm seeing. She squeezes my hand back to reassure me but doesn't turn. She's leaning up to say something to my dad, who is also not paying attention to what I see. I reach for his belt with my other hand.

"Dad," I try to whisper. But my throat is so dry and tight that all I can do is croak and he doesn't hear me. He's too busy listening to Mom.

The man with the binocular eyes is staring right at me. I can't see his mouth under that ski mask, but I think he is grinning now. He waves his hand at me and then reaches into his coat pocket to pull out something that looks like a cell phone. Then he begins to stand up, unfolding himself from his chair, and I can see how thin he is, how very tall he is. I want to scream, but I can't.

He holds that cell phone up and then, with his other hand, he presses the buttons. Once, twice . . . and there is the muffled sound of a distant explosion. The lights flicker and everything is plunged into total darkness.

14

HELP

I CAN HEAR THE sound of water dripping but I can't see anything. I seem to be lying on the ground. My head is spinning and aches horribly. I try to lift my hands up to my forehead, but they seem to be caught behind my back. I struggle to free them and realize that my wrists are stuck together. How did this happen? I'm not thinking clearly. I try to remember and the effort is too much for me. I feel as if a hole is opening up underneath me and I'm slipping into it. Just before I drop back into an unconscious state I realize that my hands are tied and that I've been taken captive—and that I know who my captor is.

"Help," I whisper, just before I fall into total darkness. "Help me."

I open my eyes again. This time I can see. Whatever was covering my eyes is gone. So is the sound of dripping water. I don't know where I was before, but I know it is not where I am now. I'm no longer afraid. Strange as it sounds, I feel peaceful. I'm somewhere down in the earth and there is gold all around me. I don't mean the color gold. I mean real gold. The walls, the floor, even the ceiling of this place is made up of veins of pure gold.

But seeing it this way, I don't feel like I'm looking at riches. I feel as if I am looking at the bones of Mother Earth, seeing them as they should be seen, hidden away. I remember reading about how some Mexican Indians believe that digging gold from the earth always hurts the land, that it is a source of strength when it remains where it is, that we humans were only meant to use whatever gold we find washed out to us in the streams. And that we should then use it only to make things of beauty, because it is a blessing.

"Little Sister," a voice says from behind me, "I am glad that your heart understands this."

I know that voice. It's Corazón. I turn to look and know something else right away. I am in one of my dreams. For instead of a short Mayan woman in her twenties wearing the inconspicuous clothing of a hotel employee, the figure that stands—or, rather, floats—before me is in no way either small or ordinary. She is the exact image that had come to my mind at the party when I tried to imagine Corazón in traditional garb. From the quetzal-plumed crown on her head to the jaguar-skin robe and the anklets of gold, she is the image of someone who is more than an ordinary human being.

I don't ask her who she is. I know that she is the one who loves children, who opens that bridge between those who breathe and those who have passed from this life.

"Little Sister," she says again. Her lips are not moving, but I hear her voice, spoken inside my head. "I have come to help you against the evil one who seeks to do you harm. He thinks this Day of the Dead is his time for revenge. He thinks he will gain power from this time when the darkness of night grows stronger. But he is wrong. He is no friend of either the living or the ancestors. He will get no help from *los muertos*."

Her breathless words give me hope. But I wonder why she is the one who has come into my dreams to help me. Where is the rabbit that has been my guide in the past?

The Lady smiles. It is a smile that doesn't just end at her face but continues to send a glow of warmth that fills the air and touches me and gives me energy. "Little Sister," she says, "your friend is known to our people, too. We know him as the quick little one who can be killed by the touch of a stick yet uses his wits to defeat those who are greater in strength. He is a great helper. It is good that Rabbit has chosen to be your friend."

She gestures around her. "This time, though, I am the one who has come to help. This is my time, my season, and this festival is mine. Even though they do not fully understand what they are doing, those who have brought this festival here have summoned me." She smiles again and drifts closer to me. "Yes, in human miles it is a long way from Mexico. But this is all one land, and the heartbeat of the earth, *el latido del corazón de tierra*, sounds everywhere."

The Lady reaches down a hand to touch me. "You will wake up now," she says. "You will know what to do. Your enemy's weakness is his own thirst for revenge. I do not promise you success, but I promise you the chance to succeed if you behave with courage. Adios."

She lifts her hand from my shoulder and, with a sudden flicker like when a movie ends and the theater goes dark, she and the place where she stood—or floated—are gone.

I'm awake. Really awake this time. I'm not in some groggy semiconscious state or in a dream. I can hear water dripping again and it is still dark because something is over my head. I'm covered by a heavy blanket and my wrists are still tied.

It all comes back to me then, everything that

happened when the lights went out. The sky had been clouded over, so there was no glow from the moon or the stars, just deep, deep dark. There was a moment's silence and then chaos. Kids were yelling—some screaming in panic and others just yelling because that is what little kids do when all the lights go out. People were shouting at one another, some telling everyone to be calm, others calling out the names of their children or their husband or their wife. People were pushing and someone fell in between me and Mom and I lost her hand. I reached for my father's belt, but it wasn't there.

I was being moved one way and then another by the surge of the crowd. It was like being caught in a riptide. But that was not the worst part. I knew that somewhere in this panicked human wave there was one being who was as calm and focused as a great white shark. I knew who had caused the lights to go out. What he had held in his hands must have been not a cell phone but a device somehow used to knock out all of the power to Mohonk Mountain House, including any backup generators. And those binocular-like things he had pulled down over his eyes were not part of a costume. I now recognized them as night-vision goggles, because my dad had a pair. While everyone else was blind, Skeleton Man could see.

I knew he was coming toward me and I knew I had to hide. I fell to my knees and crawled through the crowd of confused people, hoping that I had dropped out of his sight. I remembered seeing a table nearby and hoped I was going in the right direction. When my head hit the table leg hard I knew I'd found it. I was half-stunned and worried that I'd cut myself and that blood was dripping down my forehead, but I still pulled myself under the table as far as I could and hoped I was hidden.

But I wasn't.

Two hard, bony hands fastened on my shoulder and pulled me forward. I tried to strike out, but a terribly strong, bony arm wrapped around me, pinning my arms to my sides. I started to scream for help, but my scream was cut off by a moist cloth that was pressed over my mouth and my nose and after that there was nothing to remember other than that last moment of terror, knowing that I had been taken captive by Skeleton Man.

Until now. Until waking up to the sound of water dripping. I move just a little bit to curl myself into a ball. Then I pause. I don't sense anyone watching me, but he might be here. Listen, I think. Listen. I listen hard, but I don't hear anything other than *drip, drip-drip, drip, drip-drip*, the sound of melting snow falling on stone.

I decide it's safe to move. I bring my knees up as far as I can and thrust my bound hands down below my heels. I have to rock back and forth and it's really hard because my ankles are taped together too. But there's just enough room and I manage to squeeze my legs through and thrust them back. Now my hands are in front of me and I can bring them up to my mouth. There is another piece of tape over my mouth. It hurts, but I manage to peel the tape half-way off with my fingers. And now I can get at the tape around my wrists with my teeth. I find a loose edge and pull, then spit it out, grab again, and pull. I'm unwrapping it only an inch at a time and the taste of the tape is making me feel sick, but I don't stop. I keep at it. *Grab, pull, spit.* There's nothing else in my world but my teeth and this tape around my wrists. I can't stop, because I don't know how long I have before Skeleton Man comes back.

At last I get down to the final wrap. It is stuck so hard to the skin of my wrists that it burns as I pull it free, but I don't even pause. I reach down to my ankles and unwind the tape from them as well. They aren't as tightly wrapped as my hands were. Maybe Skeleton Man ran out of tape. Maybe he wasn't as totally prepared as he thought he was. Maybe he had underestimated me again, as he did when I escaped him the first time.

But I don't throw the blanket off right away. There is a little hole in it and I put my eye up to it and look. I can see through it just enough to make out where I am. It looks like a cave with a tunnel leading into darkness. Someone, and I know who that someone is, has been using this place for quite a while. There's a cot against one wall with a Coleman lantern next to it, and a hot plate and containers of food. To one side of the cot are shelves piled with wires and boxes and electronic equipment. The equipment is connected by a cable to several large storage batteries on the floor. There's a table on the other side of the cot, close to the mouth of the tunnel. A cell phone is sitting on that table. My cell phone. If I get it, I can call my parents, call for help.

But before I can move to throw off the blanket, I hear the scrape of a boot against rock. And through the hole in my blanket I see a ski-masked face wearing a pair of night-vision goggles appear in the mouth of the tunnel. Skeleton Man has returned.

15

IN THE CAVE

THE TALL, GAUNT FIGURE takes three slow steps, moving like a heron stalking its prey in the shallows, ready to strike at any movement. I freeze under the blanket. As he reaches up to take the night-vision goggles from his head, I quickly push the tape back over my mouth, grab the stuck-together ball of tape I've stripped from my wrists and ankles, and thrust my hands behind my back. He is taking the ski mask off now. For a moment it seems as if the face he is uncovering is that of a skeleton, nothing but white bone.

But then I see that he has human features, that his face is the same face I have seen before. It is the harsh, sharp-featured countenance of a man who might be called old, were it not for that awful vitality in his eyes, the intensity in the set of his hard mouth. I quickly close my own eyes as he leans toward me, reaching out one hand to pull the blanket off my face.

"Hunnhhh," he growls. "Still out cold?"

I feel his fingers grasp my cheek and pinch hard, but I will myself not to react. He hasn't pulled the blanket down far enough to see that my ankles are no longer taped together. He doesn't notice that the hands I'm holding behind my back are now free. The blanket is thrown over my head again. It's dusty and some of the dust gets into my nose. It is hard, so hard, not to sneeze. But somehow I manage to control myself, to keep breathing as slowly as someone in a drugged sleep.

I can hear him moving things around. I can't see through the hole in the blanket now, but I'm not even going to try. I have to stay still. I have to wait for a chance to escape, and this is not it.

The sounds tell me that he is still moving about. I don't know how long I was unconscious. Here inside the cave I can't tell if it is day or night. But my hope is that it is night, late at night. So late that, after all his exertion, he's tired.

I direct my thoughts to him: You are tired, you are very tired. You need to rest. Go to sleep, go to sleep.

When I finally hear the sound I am waiting for, I almost sigh in relief. It is the creak of the springs of the cot. Then I hear two thuds and see in my mind's eye the boots he has pulled from his feet resting on the cave floor. The cot creaks again as he stretches out on it. I hold my breath, listening even harder. He is rolling back and forth, getting comfortable, and now his breathing is turning into a snore. I think he is asleep.

I begin to move, bringing my hands back around, pulling the blanket down from my face, just a finger's width at a time. I can see him now. He is sleeping on his side, his face turned away from me. I roll to my knees and begin to crawl across the floor of the cave.

The thought goes through my head that I should do something to him, try to knock him out, try to tie him up as he did to me. But I don't see anything I could hit him with and I have this feeling, more than a feeling, that if I tried, I would fail. He would wake up and grab me. I have to head for that tunnel. It must be the way out. I get up off my knees, the blanket still over my shoulders, and keep moving. I move slowly, the way my father taught me to move when you are stalking an animal. I don't tiptoe, but I lift my feet and put them down carefully, rolling from instep to heel with each step. As I pass the table, I reach out and pick up my cell phone with one hand and Skeleton Man's night-vision goggles with the other.

For just a moment his breathing deepens and his snoring becomes words. I freeze in midstep.

"No, not yet," he growls in his sleep. "When she is awake and can see my face. Then . . . It will be painful, yes. Piece by piece, yes. I will have my revenge piece by piece."

Then his words turn into a snarl that makes the hair stand up on the back of my neck, for it is not like the sound a human being should make. It makes me think of some huge, ravenous animal ripping at the flesh of its kill. But he doesn't roll over or sit up, and his breathing again turns into a low snore. I start moving.

When I reach the mouth of the tunnel, I quicken my pace. The passageway is dimly lit by lanterns placed every hundred feet or so. I don't look at those lights. When you move through darkness, you should never look at a light, for it will lessen your perception. But as I pass each lantern I turn it out so that the darkness I leave behind will be that much deeper and maybe that much harder for him to make his way through to follow me when he wakes up.

The passageway is very long. In all the reading I've done over the last few days about the Shawangunk Mountains, I've found no mention of a cave like this, and I wonder how he found it. Is it a place where he's been before? And if so, how long ago was it when he was here last? A year ago, ten years, or at a time when he was one of those monsters that the Lenape people warned their children about in the time before the coming of the Europeans? Another hundred feet, another lantern. I'm climbing now as the floor of the passageway slopes up. There are no more lanterns, but I don't have to put on the night-vision goggles. A circle of light glows from the mouth of the cave ahead of me, and beyond that is the glitter of snow-covered earth.

When I step outside I see that the clouds have cleared from the sky. It is cold, but not the cold of deep winter. I'm warm enough with this blanket around my shoulders. The full moon is shining down. I've never welcomed the sight of the moon more than I do right now.

"Thank you, Grandmother," I say to the moon in a soft voice. As I smile at it, it seems I can see more clearly than ever before the shape that our old people remind us can sometimes be seen on the moon's face. It is Rabbit, who leaped up there long ago. He's looking down and helping me too.

I'm not sure where I am. There are thousands of acres in the Shawangunk range with no roads, just foot trails leading through the forest, up and down the ridges and cliffs. But I do see how I was brought here. Parked in front of the mouth of the cave is a bone-white four-wheel-drive all-terrain vehicle. It's the first one I've seen since we came to Mohonk. Motorized vehicles like snowmobiles and ATVs are strictly forbidden in the Mohonk Preserve. But the cover of the storm must have made it possible for him to sneak this in. The cave is at the bottom of a cliff that rises above me. Tracks in the snow lead back from the cliff down into the woods.

I've driven ATVs before. But when I look close at this one, I see I'm not going to go anywhere on it. The key is gone from the ignition. It must be in Skeleton Man's pocket.

I lift up my cell phone, thinking I can find out if my parents are okay and tell them I need help. I notice that the little phone seems even lighter than usual and I open up the back of it. The battery has been taken out.

And that is when I hear an angry, awful shriek from inside the cave. Skeleton Man has woken and discovered that I'm gone.

THE CLIFF

W HEN THE GLACIERS RECEDED from here fourteen thousand years ago, they left behind a landscape of cliffs and valleys and peaks. Over the centuries, massive chunks of rock fell off the mountains to make huge piles of stones. Those talus piles are everywhere in the Shawangunk range. Rock climbers come from all over the world to scramble through the stones and scale the sheer rock cliffs. Mom and I had taken the trail across Rhododendron Bridge onto Undercliff Carriage Road a day ago to watch some of them working their way up the Trapps Cliffs. They were so high up that on their climbing ropes they looked like tiny spiders, strung together by thin strands of web.

The memory of watching those climbers may seem like a strange thing to have going through my mind now. A part of me wants to run as fast as I can. But running would not be a good idea. I don't know the trails here and I am sure he does. I can't use the ATV, but I'm sure he has the key and can use it to pursue me. I wish I had a knife so I could cut the tires. I don't have time to open it up and do something to the engine.

But I do have another way to go. Up.

I tie the blanket around my neck and start scrambling up the huge stones that lay around the mouth of the cave, concealing it from the sight of any casual passerby. The snow makes the rocks slippery, but my moccasins are the real old-time kind, with one exception. When my mother made them, she built in arch supports and glued on durable soles that have a good tread on them. They are not just made for dress but for dancing or walking—or climbing.

I've climbed at least seventy feet before he comes out of the cave. I'm not looking back over my shoulder or down. It isn't wise to do either when you are climbing by daylight and even more foolish when you have only moonlight to show you where to find hand- and footholds. But I just know he is there. I can feel his hungry, inhuman eyes staring up at me. It is a good thing I can sense him there, because the scream that comes from his throat is so eerie, so piercing, that it might otherwise have shocked me into missing a handhold, losing my grip, and falling.

"Aaaaaarrryyyyaaaaahhhh!"

It sends a chill down my back that is much colder than the feel of the stone cliff on my bare hands. I freeze for just a second. The night-vision goggles that are perched on my forehead slip off and fall down the slope. I hear them strike rock and shatter. But I don't lose my balance or my focus and I start climbing again.

Something hits the cliff next to my face with a hard *thwack*, sending a sharp shard of stone across my cheek. I scramble up even faster and the next softball-size stone that he throws hits near my feet, the third strikes an arm's length beneath me. The fourth hits even lower than that. I think I'm out of his range now, but I don't slow up. If one of those stones had struck me, it would have knocked me loose, like a little bird struck by the spin of a throwing stick. From this height, I would not have survived a fall like that. Skeleton Man is not trying to catch me—now he wants to kill me.

The thing about rock climbing, though, is that you really can't hurry. If you do, you make mistakes. You have to be sure of your holds, certain that you haven't wedged your foot on a shelf of rock that is loose, and grasp firmly before you try to pull yourself up. We have a new climbing wall at our school and I've spent more than my share of time on it. So you might think I would be more sure of myself. But I'm not. I don't have a harness and a line on me. I don't have a chalk bag that I can dip into to keep my hands dry. I'm climbing at night on a rock face that is partially covered with snow. And I haven't even had time to study this cliff I'm scaling, to eyeball it to pick out the best route. I'm climbing blind. But I don't have any other choice.

There are plenty of loose places on this rock face, places where if I put my weight on the flat stone, it would lever out and fall, taking me with it. The thought goes through my mind that it might start a rockfall that would come down on top of him. But it isn't worth the risk if it means I have to go with it. So each time a spot starts to give as I brush away the snow and begin to put my weight on it, I quickly move my hand or my foot to another, safer hold.

Grandmother Moon is helping me. Her light is so bright on the cliff wall that I can see things pretty well. Even the angle of the shadows she casts is just right to show me where I have to put one hand and then the next. I keep making steady progress. I think I am more than halfway to the top. I no longer hear stones striking the wall beneath me. Nor does Skeleton Man let loose another scream of hunger and rage and frustration. And that silence worries me. I begin to wonder if he has a weapon of some kind, like a gun, and if he's getting it out of the ATV now. If he does, will I feel the bullet strike me before I hear the crack of the shot?

What I hear next, though, is not a gunshot. It is the roar of a motor. Skeleton Man has started up the ATV. I pause in my climb to listen as the sound moves away. Then I start climbing again. As much as I hope he's giving up and going away, something inside me says that he isn't. He knows where my climb is going to take me. He is going to cut back around to find the trail that will lead him there. When I get to the top, will Skeleton Man be there waiting for me?

THE ROAD

THE LAST FIFTY FEET of my climb are the
worst. The cliff begins to slope out and I
have to find a way around the small overhang that is above me, that is between me and where
I think the top must be. My hands are getting so
numb from grasping the snow-chilled rocks that my
fingers feel as if they are made of stone themselves.
I hold on with one hand and put the other into my
armpit. That's the warmest place on your body and

it helps restore feeling to my fingers, along with an aching pain so sharp that I almost cry out. I'm feeling exhausted, too, almost too tired to keep hanging on. I have to do something now or I'm going to fall.

Somehow, I don't really understand how, I manage to find a firm enough hold to reach one arm out and up, over the top of that overhang. My fingers find a tree root and I grab hold. It seems firm enough. I can't see it, but I think it is a cedar root. Old cedars grow strong on cliff edges. I feel as if that root is speaking to me, telling me to trust it. I have no other choice. I let go with my other hand, push out and up with my feet, and manage to get my other arm over the top as well to grasp that same friendly root. My feet are kicking at nothing but air. There's a fall of at least a hundred feet below me. I pull, wriggling my body up through snow and twigs and scree. My knees are over the edge now and I'm going hand over hand up that root, which just grows drier and firmer.

My arms wrap around the tree itself. It is as big around as my father's waist and I feel for a moment as if the old cedar tree is holding me just as much as I am holding it. Its rough bark is warm and dry against my cheek and I can smell that aroma that only a cedar has, a clean, faintly sweet scent that makes me think of healing. I remember all the times my dad or my mom and I have sprinkled dry cedar needles on glowing coals and bathed ourselves in the smoke that rose up, cleansing ourselves from all the bad influences that have touched our lives, clearing away sickness, clearing the air. My parents did that for me after the first time I escaped from Skeleton Man.

That thought takes away whatever sense of safety and security I'd been feeling. Where is he? I listen hard, and to my relief I can still hear the faint growl of an ATV. It continues to move away, not yet going upslope and coming closer. But I can't wait here. There's no time to rest. I have to keep moving. I stand up and brush the snow and dirt from my knees, slip off my moccasins to clean the grit out of them, and slide them back on again. My toes feel numb and I stomp my feet on the ground to try to bring some feeling back into them. Moving. I have to keep moving.

There's a gentle slope ahead of me. It will be easy to climb. But before I go, I place both of my hands on the trunk of the cedar whose root was my lifeline.

"Thank you, Grandfather," I say.

At the top of the slope the ground levels off to a narrow white carpet of snow that extends to my right and my left. It is so level that I know what it must be. I brush away the snow with my foot. It is the surface of a road. I look around and recognize where I am. Although the night and the snow make everything look different, I am on the main road that leads up to the Mountain House, just past the Mountain House Gate.

That road gives me both hope and a deep sense of foreboding. I can follow it back up to where there are people who can protect me. Or I can head back down toward the gatehouse. But I don't know if anyone will be there. At night, I think, they just leave it unattended, especially when there's been a big snowstorm like the one we just had and there's no likelihood of anyone driving up or down. And if I reach the gatehouse and it is all locked up and no one is there, what good will it do me? Who will protect me from Skeleton Man if he tracks me there? I might even run into him coming up the road as I am going down.

But even if I do go up, toward the Mountain House, it won't be easy. I think it is at least a mile. I can't run fast on a road slippery with snow. Skeleton Man may be able to catch up to me before I can reach safety.

I have to decide. As I stand there trying to decide what to do, I can feel myself getting colder. The blanket is still tied around my shoulders, but it is not enough to keep me from developing hypothermia if I stand still. Running—not headlong but at a careful, steady jog—will warm me up and, perhaps, get me to the place I have to reach in time. I turn and start running up the road.

18

THE BLADE

THE SNOW IS NOT as deep as it was when it first fell. The road surface must not have dropped down to freezing, so the drifts have begun to melt from the bottom. In places where it was swept by the wind, the road is actually clear of snow, but in others there is still as much as six inches with icy patches in between. So I have to run with care. I don't want to fall and hurt myself, maybe twist an ankle. I have to keep going.

253

The running is warming me up. My breathing has settled into an even, steady rhythm. But I'm far from relaxed, because I keep listening for a sound from behind me, the sound of the engine of an ATV. Every now and then I catch it as I turn round a bend. It is still thin and distant, like the whining buzz of a hornet, but I think it has been growing louder and closer. My feet thump on the road surface, then slosh through snow that is wet and heavy and pulls at my moccasins. I slip and almost fall, but I manage to catch myself with my hands and keep running.

The back of my left hand is hurting, though. I glance at my knuckles. The moonlight is bright enough to see a dark flow welling out from a cut. I don't know when that happened. Maybe it was when I was climbing and my hands were too numb to feel it, too cold to bleed freely. My near tumble has just opened it enough for the blood to start dripping out. There's a deep pocket in my buckskin dress and I reach into it with my other hand to pull out a Kleenex that I'd wadded in there. I wrap it over my bleeding knuckle. It's not that it is cut deeply enough for me to lose enough blood to weaken me. A knuckle cut doesn't bleed all that much. It is that I don't want to leave a blood trail behind me. Even though the logical part of my mind knows that the man who posed as my uncle and took me captive is just an evil human being, another part of my mind knows with equal certainty that he is more than that. He is a monster, the kind of monster that can smell blood.

I wish that I was the one on the ATV and that he was the one on foot. It's not right. In the old stories the monsters don't use machines. It isn't fair. Yes, I know it is crazy for me to think of this when I'm running for my life. But exhaustion and fear can bring thoughts into your head that don't make logical sense, like feeling there has to be some better way for me to escape other than on foot.

Then as I see a familiar cutoff in the road and a pile of earth and stone ahead of me at the cliff's edge, I realize that my thoughts are logical after all. I jog off the road to the bulldozer I had spotted the other day. On the radiator grille is a word that my dad spelled out for me when I was four years old and visiting a job site with him for the first time: INTER-NATIONAL. That word brings a smile to my face. I know this big yellow machine. My dad taught me all about it.

There's not much snow on the bulldozer, which had clearly not quite finished its work on the road before the snowstorm hit. It is still sitting here, ready to go. I step up onto the push arm and then the track to get into the cab. It isn't a really big bulldozer, but it is big enough for me to feel pro-tected by it as I step over the steering levers and sit down on the black padded seat. It is completely dry inside. I run my hands over the controls of the big machine, reminding myself what is what. The blade control lever is to the side of the right arm-rest, the decelerator—no, the brake pedal—is under my right foot. I put my hands on the two steer-ing levers, which are between my legs. Here's the decelerator pedal—under my left foot. Now . . . the engine speed control lever is by my left elbow. Yes. And the transmission shift? Okay, here it is, a foot farther to the left, over the gearbox.

I make sure everything is set, then reach my right

hand down to the starter switch.

Baabaaabaabaa-barooooom. The engine catches and then grumbles into life. I feel as much as hear the steady, smooth rumble of the big diesel as it warms up.

The instrument panel is lit now and I flick on the headlights, then work the blade control lever. There's a slight jolt as the lift cylinders pull back and the blade lifts free. I manipulate the lever to shake loose the dirt and snow. It's a good two feet off the ground, high enough so that it won't catch anything, but I can still see over it.

I push forward on the right steering lever, pull back on the left, and the bulldozer makes a tight pivot. Its headlights illuminate the snow-covered road that leads toward the Mountain House. Those lights also reflect off the bone-white finish of the ATV that has just pulled up to block my way. In the stark gleam of the headlights I can see the tall, thin figure astride that ATV, his head a glistening skull, his eyes red as blood.

19

CAT AND MOUSE

AAAAARRRYYYYAAAAAHHHH!"

Skeleton Man stares into the bright glare of the bulldozer's headlights. He has raised himself up from the seat and is standing on the ATV. He is just about to get off. He'll be on me in half a dozen strides of his long legs. The sound of the diesel motor of the bulldozer is so loud that I didn't hear his approach. I'm frozen at the controls.

But I stay frozen for only a heartbeat. I haven't

climbed and run this far to get caught like a foolish little mouse backed into a corner by a cat. Not when this mouse has several tons of steel under her, steel controlled by an engine with as much power as a herd of horses. I shift into reverse, and the bulldozer rolls backward as I work the steering levers to keep my enemy in the beam of the headlights. I hear the familiar *beep-beep-beep-beep* warning sound that echoes through every construction site whenever some big piece of machinery starts backing up. I love that sound, and right now it makes me feel as if it is the voice of this huge yellow beast I'm riding.

"Come on, baby," I say to the bulldozer as I steer her backward in a half circle. "Let's show him what you've got."

I can tell that I've surprised Skeleton Man. He probably hadn't expected a kid to be able to run a dozer. Instead of getting off the ATV, he settles back into the seat, grips the handlebars, and revs the engine so hard that when he pops the clutch it roars forward into a wheelie. But as soon as he gets close enough, I stop, shift, and roll forward even faster than I went back. Skeleton Man has to turn sharply and speed up to avoid getting hit by the blade of the dozer.

"Yes!" I say.

I'm not frightened now. There is so much adrenaline pumping through me that I feel as if I could make my big yellow metal horse take flight. I pull the left steering lever back and push forward on the right. The bulldozer spins in a tight circle so that I keep Skeleton Man in the beam of the headlights. Every time the lights catch him, he raises a bony hand to block his eyes from their glare and I can't see his full face. But what I do see makes me swallow hard. He doesn't seem at all human anymore—he's just a glaring, red-eyed skull.

It's like a dance now. Each time he tries to get close I back up, turn, roar forward, and turn again to evade his approach. I'm not certain what he thinks he'll be able to do. He must know that he can't get off his much-smaller machine to try to attack me on foot. There's no way he's going to scale the treads of a moving bulldozer. I turn, go forward, back up, spin, drive forward again.

Our game of cat and mouse continues. Though

it is more like lion versus elephant, I think. Then it comes to me. His plan isn't really to get close enough to catch me. He's trying to get me to make a mistake, stall out, or even run out of fuel. Then he can leap up into the cab and grab me like an owl sinking its claws into a baby bird. I'm safe only as long as I don't do something wrong. As soon as I think that, my wet moccasin slips off the pedal. I lurch forward out of control for a second before I manage to get my foot back in place again, my heart pounding at the thought of him catching me.

Suddenly I know—I'm seeing it wrong. I'm not the mouse. I'm the cat. I shouldn't be evading him. I should be on the attack. As quickly as I realize this, I act. I lower the blade, shift, push the throttle to its highest point, and pop my feet off the pedals. My yellow behemoth doesn't just roll forward, it seems to almost jump through the air. And it takes Skeleton Man totally by surprise. He tries to turn his ATV, but he's too late. The blade catches the side of his four-wheeler. As I raise the blade, it lifts him and his ATV up into the air.

But I've been so intent on catching my enemy off

guard that I haven't noticed where I am. I'm heading right toward the edge of the cliff! I ram the pedals to brake just as one side of the bulldozer blade hits the edge of a huge slab of rock.

Ker-whomp!

The sound of the blade hitting that huge stone is like an explosion. It's helped me stop, but it jolted me so hard that I've been thrown forward against the steering levers. The breath has been knocked out of me and I feel as if my ribs are cracked. But I can't think of that now. I slam my feet back down on the decelerator and the brake to keep from crawling forward again just as a terrible scream fills the air.

"Aaaaaarrryyyyaaaaahhhh!"

Skeleton Man and his ATV were flipped forward off the blade of the bulldozer when we struck that stone. In the beam of the headlight I see him there at the cliff's edge, the machine on top of him as he windmills his long arms, screaming as he tries to get free.

"Aaaaaarrryyyyaaaaahhhh!"

Then the earth collapses beneath him. He and the four-wheeler fall over the edge. That huge stone

I struck, which is twice the size of the bulldozer, also begins to slide. Half of the mountain slope and a big chunk of the road edge in front of me go with it.

For a second the whole world is filled with the rumble and roar of a landslide. The bulldozer shakes beneath me and I wonder if the road is going to collapse under us. But then, as suddenly as it began, it is over. As the last echoes die away, all is quiet aside from the rattle of a few stray rocks falling.

I take a deep breath. Then, holding my side, I climb off the yellow bulldozer. I leave it in neutral with its motor running, just in case. But when I get to the edge of the crumbled cliff, I can feel in my heart there's nothing to fear now. Grandmother Moon is shining her light even brighter than before on the white stones of the talus slope. She shows me that Skeleton Man is gone. He is down there somewhere, buried forever under thousands of tons of rock.

20

BY THE FIRE

A HAND GRASPS MY shoulder.

"More hot cocoa, Molly?" my mom asks. Dad is leaning over her to hold out a plate of cookies. It's teatime at the Mohonk, and we're sitting in the Lake Lounge by the fire, in the same room where the lights went out two nights ago and Skeleton Man took me away. We've had to stay here an extra two days because of the investigation, but we've managed to make most of it feel like a vacation. It hasn't been hard to enjoy ourselves now that the sense of foreboding that hung over us like a sword on a thin thread is gone.

"Thanks," I say. I reach out one bandaged hand for the cocoa and grab three cookies with the other. My parents both laugh.

"Well," I say, "I'm hungry." That makes them laugh harder and I laugh with them, even though laughing makes my bruised ribs hurt.

As we sit and look at the fire, it seems as if all the scary and awful things that just happened occurred ages ago. My fears that my parents had been hurt turned out to be groundless. That night when Skeleton Man killed all the power on the mountain, I was the only person he attacked. I'm sure he had further plans, but we'll never know what they were.

They haven't been able to find any trace of his body, though they did find some pieces of the shattered ATV at the bottom of the slope. The stones that slid down are too big for anyone to move and the state troopers say that we might as well think of it as the grave of the unidentified man who kidnapped me. From what I told them and from the way he operated, they agreed it might very well have been the same person who kidnapped my mom and dad and posed as my uncle a year ago. But with no hard evidence other than what I said I saw, that remains only a theory as far as they are concerned.

But what about that cave and all his stuff, you ask? They listened to my description of that place and they've searched for it. But the snow had all melted away by the time they started looking and they couldn't even find the tracks of the ATV. So far they haven't been able to find the cave either. I'm not sure how hard they've tried. Apparently everyone who knows anything about this area says there is no such cave that anyone else has ever found. I was probably in shock and remembered it wrong—or at least that's what they theorize. I even told them about the cedar tree whose roots helped me climb those last few feet over the cliff, but they claim there are no cedar trees growing along that stretch of road at all, and never have been.

Some things can never be explained. One of them is Corazón. My mom and I both remember meeting her and talking with her. I know she was my friend. Her face was one of those I looked for in the crowd of people gathered inside the Mohonk when I came walking up the snowy road that night—well, more limping than walking. And I think I did see her at the edge of the light from the flashlights. She was dressed again in those beautiful traditional Mayan clothes.

I saw her smile at me, put her hand on her heart, and mouth words that I am sure were *net tsoi*. I'd never heard those words before, but somehow I knew they meant "all is good" in Mayan. Then Mom and Dad were hugging me so hard that all I could see or think about was how happy I was that we were all together and safe. When I looked around again, Corazón was nowhere to be seen.

But yesterday, when Mom and I went looking for Corazón after I'd finished my first interviews with the state troopers, we couldn't find her. And when we asked, we were told that there was no one by that name employed by the Mohonk Mountain House. Mom and I just looked at each other when we heard that. Then Mom finally told me the proverb that Corazón had shared with her. "Take heart when you feel lost, for a friend may find you."

So, that's the end of my story. I'm the girl who got away from a monster not just once but twice. Even though they say that lightning doesn't strike twice, I know now that it does. I know that just as surely as I know that love and courage are strong enough to defeat hatred and greed.

And I also know Skeleton Man is gone again from our lives. This time, I hope, he is gone for good.

ACKNOWLEDGMENTS

While these two stories are novels, largely drawn from my own imagination, they would not have been possible without the many lessons I learned from such Haudenosaunee (Iroquois) elders as Tehanetorens/Ray Fadden and Dewasentah/Alice Papineau. Though they have walked on, their teachings continue.

More frightening books by
JOSEPH BRUCHAC!